Sherlock Holmes, Fantômas, Lupin Raffles and More: The Spanish Plays

FROM THE SAME AUTHOR

Sherlock Holmes, Fantômas, Lupin Raffles and More: The Spanish Plays

Plays by
**Gonzalo Jover & Emilio G. del Castillo,
Jose Maria Martin de Eugenio,
And Heraclio S. Viteri & Enrique Grimau
del Mauro**

Introduced and adapted by
Frank J. Morlock

A Black Coat Press Book

ISBN 978-1-61227-584-0. First Printing. January 2017. Published by Black Coat Press, an imprint of Hollywood Comics.com, LLC, P.O. Box 17270, Encino, CA 91416. All rights reserved. Except for review purposes, no part of this book may be reproduced or transmitted in any form or by any means, electronic or mechanical, including photocopying, recording, or by any information storage and retrieval system, without permission in writing from the publisher. The stories and characters depicted in this novel are entirely fictional. Printed in the United States of America.

TABLE OF CONTENTS

Introduction

Stumbling through the archives.

My career as a translator began unexpectedly when I was browsing through the French stacks at the University of Maryland. It was around 1980; I was teaching a class in Legal Research and had assigned some research during class time in the Mckeldin library. With nothing pressing to do until the students returned, I wandered around until I found myself with a small leather-bound book in my hand. It dated from around 1715 and the pages were of beautiful quality. It was a book of short plays by a writer named Dufresny—a French writer I'd never heard of.[1] It looked interesting, so I found a seat and started to read. I thought the play I read was possibly the funniest play I'd ever read. Simple French. It was about a woman whose only purpose in life is to make other members of her family as miserable as possible. The book probably should have been in the Rare Books Department, but it wasn't and, being a faculty member, I had the right to check it out.

After reading several of the plays, and doing a little research, I came to the conclusion that the plays had never been translated into English, and that someone really ought to do so. I concluded that that someone would be me. Fools rush in where angels fear to tread.

---

[1] Playwright Charles Dufresny, Sieur de la Rivière (1648-1724).

The play I chose was only twenty five pages long. A translation would be, I thought, a piece of cake. It took me two months to finish it! I learned the hard way that literary translation is not easy. But I am stubborn and like to complete work once I have begun. Once I did this play, other translations became easier. I found I enjoyed the work, especially discovering writers and works that had long been forgotten.

I wanted to translate works that were out of copyright so at first I stuck to 18th century plays. I discovered the University of Maryland had a very fine collection of old French plays. Then, I learned that Johns Hopkins had a good collection, too. And after that, and best of all but far away, Yale. After a few years, every time I drove up to see my mother in Boston, I would stop at Yale and spend an afternoon copying plays.

All this was before the Internet became a source. Eventually, I moved to Mexico. There, someone told me about the Internet Text Archive. It had around a million books on line and I found I was able to obtain lots of books that were unavailable, even at Yale and my other favorite libraries.

As of April 3, 2016, that number has increased to 9.6 million, with over 350,000 French titles. I also discovered the French Gallica (with at least 2 million texts), and The Bavarian Library. So a lot is available on my desktop that, as recently as a decade ago, I would have had to travel to Europe, and many libraries throughout the U.S, to obtain.

Meanwhile, I began to run out of plays that I knew I wanted to translate;

So I am constantly on the lookout for more. And when I'm not writing or translating, I enjoy searching the Internet and these sites. The sites are constantly adding new books.

Being interested in Sherlock Holmes, Raffles, and other popular characters, I periodically run searches on their names. Sometimes, I run searches on publishing houses e.g. Michel Levy Frères, Hetzel, etc. And I find new material that seems interesting. I don't know in advance what it is, but I'll find it.

And that is exactly what happened here. I've written several Sherlock Holmes plays of my own, and translated others from the French as well. I've wanted to find a Fantômas play. There's one by Gabriel Timmory, but it seems never to have been published. Nonetheless, I run searches periodically on these titles.

I was surprised a couple years ago when I discovered that there were several Spanish plays from around the time of World War I featuring Holmes, Raffles, and Fantômas. Living in Mexico, I've been learning Spanish. In order to upgrade my Spanish, I occasionally translate a Spanish play. However, with few exceptions, I find it hard to decide which play would be fun to translate. But when I came across the Raffles, Holmes and Fantômas plays, I knew I had something that would interest me— and, hopefully, my readers, too. I've also discovered plays about The Three Musketeers and The Count of Monte Cristo, which appear not to be simply translations of French plays on the subject. These will be translated in their turn.

I've also discovered that Spanish, unlike French, has changed a lot in the last 100 years. It's not just that I'm less familiar with Spanish than I am with French. But I find the syntax and the vocabulary far different from contemporary Spanish, and indeed, much harder to translate than French from either the 19th or even the 18th Century.

The plays themselves.

There is not a lot of information available on these plays, or the playwrights who wrote them. The writers, although they appear to have published numerous plays, never attained lasting fame, either in Spain or in translation. They were not famous, even in their day. They were not literary playwrights, and seemed barely familiar with the original English and French stories on which their plays were based.

They were, nonetheless, capable playwrights, and if they didn't even aspire to deliver good literature, they most certainly did aspire to delivering good theater.

Certainly, they were audacious, and apparently not very concerned about copyright laws. They were writing new unauthorized works about famous English and French literary characters at a time when that sort of thing was simply not done in England or France.

A pastiche is usually judged, good or bad, based on how well it recreates the ambiance of the original work. By that standard, the Holmes-Raffles plays are not very good pastiches. They do not capture either character as we know them from the works of Doyle and Hornung. It is simply the Great Detective versus the Great Burglar. More troubling are the supporting characters, which seem to be the pure invention of the authors. Gone are Dr. Watson and Bunny. Holmes has no companion, and Graziella, the street singing girl from Trieste or Naples, is Raffles' jealous and protective companion. And the criminal gang members also do not originate with Doyle or Hornung. Williams is a clumsy killer, handy with a knife, and Gibolette a slightly more sophisticated strangler. Hardly a match for Holmes. And Holmes himself is hardly the cerebral analyst we are familiar with. The only interesting character is Gibson, a street urchin, with a lot of pluck and cunning. Raffles lacks the suavity that Hornung endowed him with; he is simply an egotistical Burglar who, though daring, is not as clever as he thinks. When you consider that Raffles charm was modeled on Oscar Wilde (and Bunny on Lord Alfred Douglas) you can see how far the Spanish authors have strayed from the originals.

And the plays themselves are not mystery plays requiring a solution to a puzzle, but rather criminal action dramas, fast-paced, and containing many scenes that would keep an audience on tenterhooks.

With regard to the Fantômas plays, much the same may be said. There have been many movie adaptations of Fantômas, but the only stage version I know of was by the French playwright Gabriel Timmory, written around 1915.

Never having read the Fantômas novels, it's hard for me to compare these plays to the originals, but from outlines of plots and characters available on the internet, it appears that, once again, the plot and supporting characters are entirely the inventions of the Spanish authors. The locale for the action is London, about which the authors seem blissfully or perhaps willfully, ignorant. The legal procedures seem a blend of French and Spanish elements, but are certainly not English. If realism or authenticity were important, the plays would fail on all counts. As a glaring example, the authors seem to think that the English method of execution is by guillotine!

But critics and enthusiasts of the Fantômas plays stress their surreal quality, and that that is the basis of their appeal. If that is the secret of the success of the Fantômas novels, then this confusion of plot and characters and legal background only enhance the surreal quality of the action, and give it a dream-like quality, that, however far-fetched, make it all the more scary and unnerving. In a sense, reality has nothing to do with it. So, on that score, the Fantômas plays are effective pastiches. Add to that they are brilliant action dramas.

Acts I and II of *The Resurrection of Fantômas* are marvelously effective as theater. The same may be said of the first two acts of *The Triumph of Fantômas*. And that is about all that can be said of these plays: audacious, innovative, and wild, non-stop theater.

There is an exception to the above: *The Hollow Needle/Sherlock Holmes versus Arsène Lupin*, the last play in this collection. This play, "inspired" by the eponymous Maurice Leblanc novel,[2] is, strictly speaking, not an adaptation; nonetheless, it hews more closely to the atmosphere and character of Leblanc's novel than do the other plays. This is the Arsène Lupin we know and love. It is a more literary play than the others and the dialogue scintillates in scene after scene. Lupin is totally "in character." What he says is as important as what Lupin does.

The Sherlock Holmes character does not come off quite as well. Once Holmes is separated from his sidekick, Dr. Watson, much that is uniquely attractive about the character, is, if not absent, at least less prominent. Sherlock is an arrogant know-it-all detective, but not the larger than life cogitator who can solve insoluble prob-

[2] Available from Black Coat Press, ISBN 978-0-9740711-9-0.

lems.(Although all the other characters are in awe of him.)

Lupin is clearly identifiable with the original, Holmes less so. Possibly, because Leblanc is not as good about setting the atmosphere or portraying the eccentricities of the world's first consulting detective as was Doyle, the Sherlock of the play comes across as an accomplished, but unlikable, bloodhound, rather than an inspired, if flawed, genius. As has been pointed out by more than one critic, Holmes and Watson are not just interesting simply as detectives, because theirs is a relationship of friendship, as much as it is about this peculiarly cerebral detective.

In the end one must admire both the skill and audacity of these Spanish playwrights who appropriated both English and French characters with considerable degrees of success.

Frank J. Morlock

SHERLOCK HOLMES VS. RAFFLES

by Gonzalo Jover & Emilio G. del Castillo.
(1908)

CHARACTERS

Graziella
Betsy Weimer
Williams
Jacob
Gibolette
Gibson
Raffles
Sherlock Holmes
Inspector Hamilton
Mr. Weimer
A Street Singer
Thieves, Prostitutes, Police, etc.

The action takes place in London circa 1908.

SCENE 1

A Pub in the suburbs of London near the Thames. Night. AT RISE, Sherlock Holmes is seated in a corner, disguised as a beggar, with a pitcher of beer in front of him. Loose women, denizens of the underworld and thieves drink at the tables. Near the bar, there is a large cask, the cover of which is removed by Jacob, the innkeeper.

CHORUS:
Hurrah for the children of confusion,
In shadow, the city sleeps.
What splendid booty is kept in his hollow,
WOMEN:
Drink! Toast!
MEN: Jacob! Another cask
THIEF: You're going to get drunk.
ALL:
Pour the beer in torrents,
So as to have an unrivalled orgy.
Each time tomorrow's lost,
Is precious freedom.
WOMEN:
Drink! Toast!
Tomorrow is a mystery,
That no one has deciphered.
ALL:
Hurrah! The men of the mist.
The city sleeps in shadows.
What splendid booty is kept in its breast,
Toasting its conquest with great audacity.
WILLIAMS: Are you going to open your cask, Jacob?
JACOB: I'm going to close this one because you emptied it.
GIBOLETTE: Go ahead and serve me gin. Would you like to drink with me, Williams?
WILLIAMS: Gin is for sailors not thieves. As far as I'm concerned there are no more than two drinks. Dark beer and red wine. That's all that gets me drunk.
GIBOLETTE: Bad to get drunk. It loosens your tongue and the day you talk, you will wind up getting hanged.
WILLIAMS: Sooner or later, you must deal with it. The gallows doesn't scare me.

JACOB: Would you please not talk foolishness. It will sadden the clientele.

GIBOLETTE: Is it our future that there'll be nothing disagreeable in it?

WILLIAMS: You can see that now. There's no falling off of business. The Police watch us excessively, and Sherlock Holmes hunts down one of us every day.

GIBOLETTE: What a shrewd man.

WILLIAMS: You don't half ridicule him. He will do away with all the children of the fog if it goes on like this.

GIBOLETTE: There's one who exceeds him in shrewdness, and boasts of it.

WILLIAMS: One of us?

GIBOLETTE: Not officially. The famous Raffles—glory of thieves.

JACOB: Hurrah for the great Raffles!

ALL: Hurrah!

GIBOLETTE: Raffles has done wonders. He robbed the silversmith Levy of 20,000 pounds sterling, and he did it all by himself without leaving any track.

WILLIAMS: Jacob, make me a friend of this man and I'll get old in your tavern.

GIBOLETTE: Would he were willing! Under his direction we would be invincible. He's a genius—but he won't accept us.

WILLIAMS: He works without accomplices?

JACOB: The elect enter the honored society. It is his specialty.

(A loud whistle.)

GIBOLETTE: Silence!

(Pause. All wait anxiously.)

JACOB: It's Gibson's warning. Someone foreign to the gang is coming here. But it's not police. He's got a special whistle for them.

(Raffles enters elegantly dressed with gold glasses.)

RAFFLES (entering): Innkeeper! A pitcher of beer.

JACOB: In a moment, milord. (aside) Where did this bird come from?

GIBOLETTE (aside to Williams): Must be a banker! See—gold spectacles.

WILLIAMS: You could serve him so as to see where he keeps his purse.

GIBOLETTE (aside to Williams): You can make sure that he leaves without them.

WILLIAMS: Supposing he leaves.

JACOB: Do you want anything else, milord? Although this place doesn't look very elegant, it had great credit with the select.

RAFFLES(ironic): Of the parish?

JACOB: For the food. The best plates in London are cooked here.

RAFFLES: Bring me better beer.

WILLIAMS: Let's go swipe his purse.

GIBOLETTE: Better take it full. Wait—now's the time! All the sailors in these parts come to drink the last swallow of gin.

(Graziella enters with sailors and their girls.)

GRAZIELLA:
Everything is gay, everything is beautiful,
In the mountains of the Tyrol.
Outside of its enchantment,
Brings grief to my heart.

CHORUS:
Sweet and elegant Tyrolean,
Keep singing your song.

Be sure of it, you are envied.
It's like listening to a nightingale.
RAFFLES: Poor Graziella, in your song tears strive to appear.
GRAZIELLA:
A Tyrolean shepherd sang,
His song of love and sorrow,
And the mocking echo repeated,
How between sobs he sang,
And that I adore my beauty.
(imitating an echo)
Why you are my soul—soul.
And it is my lone star
She! She! She!
Of this passion that burns me,
Nothing deafens the call.
And the echo replies.
Soul! Soul! Soul!
CHORUS
Sing, beautiful Tyrolean,
So long as love holds the call.
GIBOLETTE
And the echo repeats its promises
Soul! Soul! Soul!
Because it is the best thing,
To keep in the soul
A bit of love.
CHORUS:
That is the best.
A nice singer
Who gives us her love.
WILLIAMS: It's a very beautiful song; but there's nothing we like better than a jig.
ALL:

Right! Right! Right!
(They all dance.)
THIEF: Jacob, bring our gin!
JACOB: I'll serve them myself.
(Goes to serve the sailors.)
WILLIAMS: Gibolette, as soon as they go—
GIBOLETTE: We will pay the caballero's bills.
WILLIAMS: By degrees or by force.
GIBOLETTE (to others): Attention, mates.
(He talks to them in whispers.)
WILLIAMS (to Graziella): What about you? you're not drinking anything?
GRAZIELLA: I'm keeping the alms they give me for my singing.
WILLIAMS: Your public ought to make you a millionaire.
GRAZIELLA: I get more from the poor than the rich.
WILLIAMS: What you should do is let yourself go soon. You're not one of us.
GRAZIELLA: I know your tricks, Williams. Don't worry. I foresee your future: You'll dance at the end of a rope.
WILLIAMS (drawing back): What!
GIBOLETTE (joining in the conversation): Graziella is a shrewd bird who works for her money, but she won't hinder you, right, beautiful?
WILLIAMS: Bah! Any way you prefer. We won't go into it.
GIBOLETTE: Be compassionate—right when you're giving a good punch.
WILLIAMS: Yes, now's the time. We're alone. Let's get him.
THIEVES: Right! Right!
RAFFLES (very calm): Is it me you're looking for?

20

WILLIAMS: No doubt. Let's not waste time. Give us your money.

GIBOLETTE: My buddy, Williams is a bit abrupt. Dish it out, Milord. The truth of the matter is we need what you've got.

RAFFLES: It exceeds my courage to keep within bounds, and I lack patience to listen. Is a man of heart robbed like this in London?

WILLIAMS: My knife wants to know if you've got one.

OTHERS: Swat the fly!

RAFFLES (seizing a stool): Try to get it from me.

WILLIAMS: Go for him!

ALL: Go for him.

(They charge Raffles. Graziella intervenes.)

GRAZIELLA: Stop! Do you know who you are treating like this?

WILLIAMS: We don't care if he's the devil himself.

GRAZIELLA: It's Raffles.

ALL (falling back): Raffles!

GIBOLETTE: The famous Raffles! Our ideal!

RAFFLES: Truly, you need even more lessons.

(He removes his disguise.)

RAFFLES: I am Raffles!

ALL: Hurrah! Hurrah!

GIBOLETTE: Dispose of us!

JACOB: Raffles visiting my establishment! Tomorrow I'll put up a new sign!

RAFFLES: Sometimes, folks like you are necessary.

JACOB: We will all serve you—but each in his own way, according to his specialty. Williams as a bravo, Gibolette with his clever hands.

RAFFLES: But who is that who doesn't seem concerned with the action?

JACOB: He's not one of us, he must be a beggar.

21

RAFFLES: Anybody know him?

WILLIAMS: I don't.

GIBOLETTE: Me, either.

JACOB: He drinks and he is quiet.

RAFFLES: Suppose he was a spy?

ALL (looking at the beggar and drawing their knives): A spy!

RAFFLES: Why not? Come here, old friend.

HOLMES: I'm just fine here. If you want something, come to me.

RAFFLES: Who are you? I suspect you.

HOLMES: That's your right.

RAFFLES: What are you here for?

HOLMES: You are impulsive and angry, Raffles.

RAFFLES: You know my name?

HOLMES: You said it yourself just now, so you'd be acclaimed. You're really a bit vain. You don't deserve your fame. If I were Holmes. you would be lost.

ALL (with fear): Sherlock Holmes!

HOLMES: I don't know Raffles personally.

RAFFLES: Now you know him.

HOLMES: Maybe.

RAFFLES (to others): Leave us alone.

GRAZIELLA: Raffles!

RAFFLES: Leave us alone. Friend or foe, this man is worthy of me.

HOLMES: Who neither fears nor admires you.

RAFFLES (to all): Beat it!

GRAZIELLA: You insist on it. But we'll be nearby. At the first call—

WILLIAMS: It would be better to act without calling anyone. Whoever he is or he isn't, a dead man doesn't talk.

HOLMES: You are mistaken Williams. Three of the men you killed identified you to the Police.

RAFFLES (imperiously): Beat it!

(All leave.)

GRAZIELLA (to Williams): Trust me, Williams. Before this beggar leaves the inn you should leave London.

(They are gone.)

RAFFLES: Now we are alone, face to face, let's talk plainly.

HOLMES: Do you need to in order to understand me?

RAFFLES: Yes.

HOLMES: Fine. Famous Raffles, it's Sherlock Holmes who's come to visit you.

(Holmes removes his disguise.)

RAFFLES and GRAZIELLA: Sherlock Holmes!

(Raffles starts to dart out, but Holmes detains him.)

HOLMES: Be calm. This attack would be the cause of your ruin. Calm down, calm down. If I'd come to take you, you'd be in cuffs.

RAFFLES: You didn't come for that?

HOLMES: No—solely to meet you.

RAFFLES: And how did you guess that I would come here today?

HOLMES: I watched your lover, Graziella. She's been coming here every night, exploring the terrain for your visit.

RAFFLES: That's true.

HOLMES: I was sure I wasn't mistaken. Unquestionably you are preparing some action that requires confederates. Bad company, you're selecting. So you see, I grieve for you. All these folks are known to the Police; they are in your line of work, but lack your genius. It's a cat and mouse game, but the feline wins sooner or later.

RAFFLES: You plan to devour me?

23

HOLMES: Difficult tasks seduce me.

RAFFLES: All I have to do is call—

HOLMES: Police surround this place; call your friends, an army of police will come.

RAFFLES: So why don't you come and get me?

HOLMES: In front of the English courts, there is no proof against you. Only I know you are an American bandit. But I'm not really concerned with putting you in jail. What's important to me is to win.

RAFFLES: So far, you haven't.

HOLMES: I will if I force you to retire.

RAFFLES: Me? Retire.

HOLMES: Either you get out of the business or you will fall into my power.

RAFFLES: Are you daring me?

HOLMES: Exactly.

RAFFLES: So far you're just boasting.

HOLMES: A thousand pounds sterling.

RAFFLES: If you can prove me guilty—?

HOLMES

You abandon your profession and leave town.

RAFFLES: If not—?

HOLMES: If I haven't caught you in six months, I'll owe you a thousand pounds.

RAFFLES: It's a deal. Easy money. When do we start?

HOLMES: Tonight. As soon as you leave here.

RAFFLES: Holmes versus Raffles. That's a struggle worthy of both of us.

HOLMES: Which I will win.

(Holmes leaves.)

GRAZIELLA: You will lose—you don't know this man.

RAFFLES: I know myself.

GRAZIELLA: I will lose you forever. (after a short pause) Let's leave England. We can be happy somewhere that Holmes cannot follow you.

RAFFLES: Bah! He was able to defy me here, but in London society where I am adored as the noble sportsman Baron Newcastle, I will win.

GRAZIELLA: But I won't be able to protect you there.

RAFFLES: No—you are my secret corner of paradise. A haven from this world of my operations.

(Graziella yells at one of the doors.)

JACOB: Is the field free?

WILLIAMS: Who was that beggar?

GIBOLETTE: No beggar. See his disguise—!

(He points to the disguise Holmes left.)

WILLIAMS: Why did you let him escape. He was a spy.

RAFFLES: Worse than that.

GRAZIELLA: He was that detective—Sherlock Holmes.

WILLIAMS: Damnation! And you didn't kill him?

JACOB (comically desperate): Holmes is my hero! Tomorrow I'll close the business.

WILLIAMS: Holmes! We are lost! For sure the Police are surrounding the tavern.

(Two whistles are heard.)

JACOB: Get out of here. I'm closing up.

WILLIAMS: Knives in hand, everybody! We must clear this door! Let's get out of here.

(Raffles rapidly puts on Sherlock Holmes' abandoned disguise. Hamilton, with police, enters.)

HAMILTON: Halt in the name of the law!

WILLIAMS: Make way. You won't take us without dead men.

JACOB (aside): Where to hide?

(He looks around for a hiding place.)

GRAZIELLA (low to Raffles): Raffles!

RAFFLES (low): Don't be afraid. I'm okay.

HAMILTON: Do you surrender? Yes or no?

WILLIAMS: No!

HAMILTON: Subdue this low life!

(The Police advance.)

GIBOLETTE: Combat mode. Save yourself if you can.

(Confusion. The thieves flee in all directions. Some escape, others are caught by the police. Jacob hides in a beer barrel and puts the top of the barrel over him. Hamilton goes to subdue Raffles. Graziella interposes herself.)

HAMILTON: Get them! Get them!

THIEVES: Flee! Flee!

HAMILTON: You won't escape, scamp!

GRAZIELLA: Get back! Don't touch this man.

RAFFLES: Stupid! Let me leave! Don't you know that Raffles, the most famous thief in London, is escaping?

(He points to the door.)

HAMILTON (to his men): It's Sherlock Holmes disguised as a beggar.

GRAZIELLA: It's Holmes. Let him pass.

(Raffles leaves.)

HAMILTON (to Graziella): Why are you meddling in this? Yours is a nice part. We will see you in Police Headquarters.

HOLMES (entering): Hamilton! Hamilton!

HAMILTON: Holmes! That wasn't you disguised as a beggar?

HOLMES: No, it was Raffles who donned my disguise.

HAMILTON: This woman said it was you, but she will pay for it.

HOLMES: Let her go.

HAMILTON: But Holmes—

HOLMES: Let her go, I said.

26

(going to her)

HOLMES: Tell your lover that I will keep the bet. The game begins.

GRAZIELLA: Holmes—

HOLMES: Get going.

(Graziella leaves.)

GRAZIELLA: Raffles will be defeated—but I will save him.

HAMILTON: Where's the thief that owns this den? How I want to nab him.

HOLMES (approaching two police men): You won't have trouble finding him. (to the police) Here, roll this barrel to the banks of the Thames and throw it in the river.

JACOB (in the barrel): Help! Help!

HOLMES (feigning surprise): Eh? There's someone inside.

HAMILTON: A wretch hiding in there? In the Thames! In the Thames!

JACOB: Help. I am Jacob the innkeeper.

HOLMES: He looks good in there. A bath wouldn't harm him.

HAMILTON: Take the rest of them to prison. The cask in the river. Close the inn. Business terminated.

(The Police roll the cask out and arrest the thieves.)

HOLMES: Now, Raffles! You and me!

CURTAIN

SCENE II

A lonely and mysterious street. In the afternoon.

(Raffles enters furtively and whistles. Short whistles answer. Williams and Gibolette appear.)

WILLIAMS: Ready for anything.

GIBOLETTE: Except escaping from fighting with the police.

RAFFLES (mysteriously): I've prepared a great strike.

GIBOLETTE: Just make sure it doesn't land on our shoulders.

RAFFLES: Fulton, the millionaire banker, is suffering from an illness; it's necessary to cure him of it.

WILLIAMS: I'm an excellent surgeon.

(He draws his knife.)

GIBOLETTE: To ease his angina, I will operate on him.

(He makes a gesture of strangling.)

RAFFLES: You only think of violent methods.

GIBOLETTE: Williams, not me.

WILLIAMS: Can you also steal?

RAFFLES: Steal, yes. Kill, never. There's nothing better than stealing. The world is made of robbers and thieves; of the stupid and the clever. Blood tarnishes money. I am an artist at stealing.

WILLIAMS: We admire you for that. Tell us what you have in mind.

GIBOLETTE: Tell us the banker's infirmity and we will manage his care.

RAFFLES: Will you promise me not to use violence?

WILLIAMS: Promised.

RAFFLES: Good. Banker Fulton suffers from intoxication with riches. He constantly worries how to employ his enormous wealth. Because his excessive work might harm him, I've decided to lighten his burden by relieving him of 100,000 pounds.

WILLIAMS: The more pounds the better.

GIBOLETTE: Explain what we must do.

RAFFLES: We're going to pay him a visit. So as not to damage the carpets of his house, we'll wear rubber shoes. The visit will be late and I don't want Mr. Fulton to be disturbed by hearing us, and come down to receive us. We will need someone agile who can scale the wall surrounding his house, and open the gate for us.

GIBOLETTE: For that, Gibson the kid who acted as lookout for us would be ideal.

WILLIAMS: We won't be late.

RAFFLES: The rest is my thing.

GIBOLETTE: No one is as ingenious as you.

WILLIAMS: Dispose of my knife.

RAFFLES: I've a much more powerful weapon: love.

GIBOLETTE: Love?

RAFFLES: Yes, Lady Betsy, the daughter of Lord Weimer, loves me madly. That love will make us rich. I'll explain later.

GIBOLETTE: I'm going to be ill with curiosity.

WILLIAMS: Silence! Here comes Gibson. (calling) Hey, Gibson.

GIBSON (enters singing, but is scared seeing Williams, and stops) Mr. Williams.

WILLIAMS: Hey, ragamuffin! Are you afraid of getting walloped for being late?

GIBSON: Me?

GIBOLETTE: Leave the poor kid in peace.

WILLIAMS: He's making fun of me.

RAFFLES: Enough! Listen kid—Williams won't wallop you if you do what I tell you.

GIBSON: What do you want me to do?

RAFFLES: Can you climb a wall 10 feet high?

GIBSON: I've done higher.

RAFFLES: Once inside you would have to open a gate.

WILLIAMS: He lost his key.

GIBSON: How much do I get?

RAFFLES: You won't complain, I promise you that. Tonight at 10, at the corner of Saint James Street.

WILLIAMS: Don't forget.

RAFFLES: And don't you forget the rubber shoes.

GIBSON: I'm going.

WILLIAMS: Goodbye. Later.

(Raffles and Gibolette leave.)

(As soon as the others have left Williams seizes Gibson planning to whack him.)

WILLIAMS: And now we are going to see if I am a brute or not.

GIBSON: Don't you hit me. Get out.

WILLIAMS: Ragamuffin. Rascal.

(Gibson runs away pursued by Williams)

GIBSON: Help! Because you are very brutish. Help!

(Enter Holmes disguised as a sailor.)

HOLMES: Bravo, bully, bravo!

WILLIAMS (turning around): Huh? Nobody called you, sailor.

HOLMES: This kid asked for help.

WILLIAMS: Leave the kid in peace and follow me.

HOLMES: I like it here.

WILLIAMS: In that case, you'll enjoy seeing me whack this ragamuffin.

HOLMES: I forbid you to do that.

WILLIAMS: Who are you to do that?

HOLMES: Someone who can.

WILLIAMS: Well, in that case instead of thrashing Gibson, I'll thrash you.

HOLMES: That will be more difficult.

(Holmes, without apparent force, subdues Williams.)

GIBSON (aside to Williams): You are going to wreck tonight's plans with this sailor.

WILLIAMS: I'll kill you if you talk.

GIBSON: Get out of here.

WILLIAMS: But...

GIBSON: Are you going, yes or no?

WILLIAMS: I'm going. Until later.

(He leaves.)

GIBSON: Who are you?

HOLMES: Sherlock Holmes.

GIBSON: You!

(Gibson would like to leave.)

HOLMES: It's useless to hide now. I know that tonight there are plans to rob the home of a banker. You will be the one to climb the wall and let the others in.

GIBSON: How do you know that?

HOLMES: It's very simple. That man is a known criminal and he'd be associating with a young punk like you only to use you as a pawn.

GIBSON: And how do you know it's a banker?

HOLMES: They're the ones with money. Other targets are jewelers, stock brokers...

GIBSON: And that they'd pick me to scale the wall?

HOLMES: In matters like these, young and agile kids are used. You are young and agile.

GIBSON: You know everything. You'll send me to prison.

(He starts to cry.)

HOLMES: That depends on you. If you are being forced into it, and want to redeem yourself, you will obey me. If you don't I'll know where to find you.

GIBSON: I'll obey you. I swear.

HOLMES: Fine. But if you try to deceive me or warn the others—

GIBSON: I'll do whatever you tell me.

HOLMES: You know Graziella—she sings in the streets?

GIBSON: Yes, mister.

HOLMES: Graziella is enamored of Raffles, a gentleman robber I'm interested in catching. Pretend to love her. And while you are at it, make her jealous of Raffles.

GIBSON: Whatever you say Mr. Holmes.

HOLMES: You think you can do it?

GIBSON: Yes, sir. Leave it to me.

HOLMES: And you will report anything you learn to me.

GIBSON: How will I find you to do that?

HOLMES: I will find you. And if you don't know how to make love to a woman, you would do well to learn.

(After Holmes leaves, Gibson resumes his cocky ways.)

GIBSON: Learn? I'm a master in such matters. I know how to manage the whores. Or make a girl into a whore. So, forward march, fix bayonets.

(Williams returns without Gibson seeing him and grabs him by the neck,)

WILLIAMS: Where do you think you are going, kid?

GIBSON: Me?

WILLIAMS: Where'd the sailor go?

GIBSON: He walked off.

WILLIAMS: Where to?

GIBSON: To his ship, or some dive, I suppose. He didn't say.

WILLIAMS: Always the wise guy, aren't you? You are going to catch it.

GIBSON: Only if you can catch me, fat ass!

WILLIAMS: Little devil!

GIBSON (after going to the corner, he turns): I believe in doing good for evil. There's a cop coming this way and he was one of those at the inn the other night. We'd both do well to get out of here.

WILLIAMS: For once you're right.

(Williams moves away running awkwardly.)

GIBSON (thumbing his nose at him): You really can move for a fat ass.

(Gibson leaves laughing.)

CURTAIN

SCENE III
THE HOUSE OF WEALTH

The ground floor of Fulton's mansion. Night. Moonlight comes through the window.

RAFFLES: Hard work for us to raise this cursed stone.

GIBOLETTE: And people say we steal because we're lazy. They should try this work.

WILLIAMS (joking): It's harder for us to steal his money than Fulton works to make it.

RAFFLES: Watch carefully. Open the window so we can get out quickly that way if we have to.

(Williams opens the window. Raffles circles the safe.)

RAFFLES: Let's proceed.

(Light from an automobile in the distance.)

RAFFLES: They cannot see us from the automobile. Is it coming here?

GIBOLETTE: No, it's heading towards London.

RAFFLES: What time is it, Williams?

WILLIAMS (looking at his watch in the moonlight): Three thirty.

RAFFLES: We need to finish quickly. (pacing around the safe) The difficulty is to figure out the combination. That may take too long.

GIBOLETTE: It makes me mad when I think of the money that must be inside.

HOLMES (emerging from the safe gun in hand): Let me spare you some trouble.

(The thieves retreat in fear.)

WILLIAMS: Damnation! Sherlock Homes!

GIBOLETTE: Curses!

HOLMES (to Police who suddenly appear): Subdue them!

(As the Police approach Raffles, Holmes stops them.)

HOLMES: No, this one is mine. Finally, you've fallen in my power.

RAFFLES (naturally, and with comic courtesy): That cheers me up infinitely. You've really surprised me greatly.

HOLMES: Pleasantly?

RAFFLES: Yes, of course. But, I beg you, nice detective, hold me by the other arm. There's an old wound in this one and the pressure hurts me.

HOLMES: It would be discourteous to deny your request.

RAFFLES: A thousand thanks!

HAMILTON (to Gibolette and Williams): In the end you fell into the mouse trap.

WILLIAMS: Bad luck. We expected to find more than 20,000 pounds in this safe.

HOLMES: Well, you found me and I'm worth more than that paltry sum.

(An automobile stops outside. Raffles becomes attentive.)

RAFFLES(to himself): The moment has come.

(With a violent jerk, he gets free leaving Holmes, stupefied, holding an artificial arm.)

HOLMES: Curses! You're wearing an artificial arm!

RAFFLES (cheerfully, as he leaps through the window): Bye, bye, Sherlock!

HOLMES: Everybody after him!

(The noise of the car pulling away can be heard)

HOLMES: Stop! It's useless. I've figured out his plan. (pointing to the window) If I could stop the car with a gunshot!

(rushing to the window he takes careful aim and fires several shots.)

HOLMES: Too late. Didn't get him. Now he's laughing at me.

HAMILTON: Shall I call ahead to the police to detain all cars?

HOLMES: No—take these gentlemen to jail. Let two men stay here to watch in case he doubles back.

(Holmes picks up the prosthetic arm)

HAMILTON: What are you going to do with that arm?

HOLMES: I'm going to keep it as a souvenir of Raffles. The mouse has lost an appendage, but this cat, you see, still has claws. Let's go, if you are ready, Hamilton.

C U R T A I N

SCENE IV
THE ITALIAN GIRL

A street in London. Night.

GRAZIELLA: I beg you, for God's sake, don't deceive me.
GIBSON: Why should I do that?
GRAZIELLA: What you are telling me about Raffles is impossible.
GIBSON: I saw him talking to her.
GRAZIELLA: Where? When?
GIBSON: This very night. Right here. He whistled, looked about, and they opened the door for him. He didn't leave until midnight.
GRAZIELLA: It's impossible.
GIBSON: You don't know how men change. The other day I went up that tree to watch them through the window.
GRAZIELLA (anxiously): And what did you see?
GIBSON: I saw them sitting on a sofa, very lovey dovey.
GRAZIELLA: Alone?
GIBSON: The father went out and they profited by it.
GRAZIELLA (dejected): My God!
GIBSON: He held her in his arms, like this. And talked to her like this. And hugged her like this.
(Gibson holds her tight.)
GRAZIELLA: Little boy.
(She pushes him away.)
GIBSON: I was just trying to give you an idea of what was going on.

GRAZIELLA: Right, right. And then what happened?

GIBSON: The girl got up, rather disheveled. She pulled the blinds and I didn't see any more.

GRAZIELLA: My God, how disgraced I am!

GIBSON: Poor thing! Poor thing! Lean on my chest, don't be stupid.

(Graziella sobs.)

GIBSON: Don't cry. I am here.

GRAZIELLA: I swear that I'll avenge myself—

(She cries some more.)

GIBSON: Go ahead, cry. (looks at his watch) He might be here any minute.

GRAZIELLA: Listen, Gibson...

GIBSON: Maybe I'd better go.

GRAZIELLA: Do you want to go?

GIBSON: I'd better.

GRAZIELLA: Then go!

(Gibson seems to leave, but hides.)

GIBSON: Let's watch the reconciliation.

(After a moment Raffles enters.)

RAFFLES: Graziella!

GRAZIELLA: Raffles!

RAFFLES: What are you doing here?

GRAZIELLA: I came to kill a doubt which prevents me from being happy.

RAFFLES: Doubts—what about?

GRAZIELLA: A doubt about—you.

RAFFLES: I've proven my love to you. Often.

GRAZIELLA: You sigh for another woman. The thought of you laughing with her at me... If it's true, I swear I'll make you suffer as I am suffering.

RAFFLES: Graziella, I love you. Trust me.

GRAZIELLA: Then where are you coming from?

RAFFLES: You know.

GRAZIELLA: Yes. You've been with a woman—and cheating on me.

RAFFLES: I have to leave you. I'm very late.

GRAZIELLA: If you go to see her, it's all over.

RAFFLES: I don't compromise with threats.

(starts to leave.)

GRAZIELLA: By the Holy Madonna, I will curse you!

RAFFLES: I laugh at your threats.

GRAZIELLA: Traitor!

RAFFLES: Bye, bye, Graziella, ha, ha, ha.

GRAZIELLA: Raffles, Raffles!

(She picks up a stone and throws it at his disappearing figure.)

GIBSON (emerging): Now do you believe me?

GRAZIELLA: Yes. Go tell the Police I will cooperate with them.

GIBSON: It would be better to tell Sherlock Holmes.

GRAZIELLA: Holmes, yes, Holmes! That would be better. Go, go!

GIBSON: I'm going.

GRAZIELLA: Why haven't you gone yet?

(Gibson leaves, chuckling.)

GRAZIELLA: Raffles, arrested. Maybe they'll hang him. No, no, that cannot be. What to do? Gibson! Gibson! (a pause) Gibson! He's gone. Forgive me, Raffles! I'm the one who ruined you. But—I will yet save you!

CURTAIN

SCENE V
A SURPRISE

An elegant room. Night. Electric lights.

WEIMER: You don't want to go to the concert?
BETSY: No, Papa. I have bit of a headache, and there's no time to dress.
WEIMER: Hmm. You are hoping Baron Newcastle will call. Do you think I haven't noticed how his visits please you?
BETSY: He pleases you, too, Papa.
WEIMER: He seems like a real gentleman—they're hard to find these days.
(Betsy fidgets. Weimer tries to decide whether to go alone when a servant enters.)
SERVANT: Sir George Darlington, Baron Newcastle.
(Weimer gestures to admit him.)
WEIMER: Ah, dear friend—
RAFFLES: Good evening. I was afraid you might have gone to the concert.
BETSY: Finally, you've come...
WEIMER: Glad you came. We we're getting bored by ourselves.
RAFFLES: I'm glad to be here. I must tell you some bandits attacked me on my way here. I was lucky to escape.
BETSY: My God!
WEIMER: Did they rob you?
RAFFLES: They got away with fifteen pounds, and a tie pin.

WEIMER: This is unheard of. I'm going to have my servants pursue them.

RAFFLES: As you please, but it's really not worth the trouble.

WEIMER: I assure you, Baron, that if we catch them, they are going to be made an example of. I'm going in pursuit.

(He leaves, Raffles goes to Betsy.)

BETSY: Are you injured? Don't hide anything from me.

RAFFLES: No, dear Betsy.

BETSY: How many robbers assaulted you?

RAFFLES (laughing): None! None at all!

BETSY: But—

RAFFLES: I needed a pretext so we would be alone.

BETSY (delighted): That was a very bad thing to do.

RAFFLES: Forgive me. I did it for you.

BETSY: Do you love me so much?

RAFFLES: With all my heart.

BETSY: I am so lucky.

(The noise of an argument is heard.)

BETSY: What's wrong?

RAFFLES (uneasily): Nothing. (aside) That was the voice of Sherlock Holmes.

BETSY: You are pale. Are you ill?

RAFFLES: It's emotion. We have so few moments together. Smell this new scent? Tell me if you like it.

BETSY: It's very strong. My God!

(She faints.)

RAFFLES: The chloroform worked fast. Luckily.

(He pulls her behind the folding screen.)

RAFFLES: Now, the silk ladder...

(He attaches a silk ladder which he takes from his hat to the window—then opens it and lets it fall.)

RAFFLES: The furniture in disarray will demonstrate that there was a struggle.

(He overturns a chair or two.)

RAFFLES: Now to hide myself. This time it's my turn, Sherlock.

(He hides in a passageway. Sherlock Holmes and Weimer enter.)

WEIMER: Incredible. To think that such a fine gentleman could be the infamous Raffles.

HOLMES: You cannot entertain the least doubt.

WEIMER (looking around): Oh, my God! He's robbed me of my daughter!

HOLMES (surprised): Is it possible?

WEIMER (goes to the open window): See the ladder by which the wretch fled.

HOLMES (calmly): Yes, I see the ladder.

WEIMER (desperate): My daughter! My daughter, Mr. Holmes!

HOLMES: It may be possible to overtake him. Order your servants to pursue him.

WEIMER: And you?

HOLMES: I will stay here.

WEIMER: I'm on my way.

(He leaves.)

HOLMES (looking around, then sniffing): It smells of chloroform... (goes to the window) That ladder. It's a false scent to distract me.... (looking at the screen) He's hiding here somewhere. That screen? No, probably Mr. Weimer's daughter is there. He's found a better place...

(He pulls out his revolver, then goes to the passageway where Raffles is hidden.)

HOLMES: Now, friend Raffles, come out of there or I shoot.

RAFFLES: I congratulate you, Sherlock.

HOLMES: Any attempt to flee will cost you your life. Spare me the violence.

RAFFLES: Cigarette?

HOLMES: No, thanks.

RAFFLES: Why not?

HOLMES: Because you've probably placed a narcotic in it. And I really don't care to fall asleep at this moment.

(Graziella climbs through the window, without Holmes seeing her. Raffles sees her but remains impassive.)

RAFFLES: It's too early to claim victory, Sherlock. I can still escape.

HOLMES: Just try!

RAFFLES: Right now.

(Raffles moves, and Graziella grabs Holmes and struggles with him as Raffles vanishes.)

HOLMES (getting loose from Graziella and grabbing her): He's escaped me, but you won't.

GRAZIELLA: I don't care. My life is his. Take it if you want it, Sherlock Holmes.

HOLMES: No, you are free. Raffles has escaped this time because your love protected him. But it's not over yet. Go, tell him he will feel the clutches of Sherlock Holmes before it is over.

(Graziella kisses Holmes who is rather shocked, and she runs away gratefully. In the distance Raffles laughter can be heard.)

CURTAIN

THE CLUTCHES OF SHERLOCK HOLMES

Part II of SHERLOCK HOLMES VS. RAFFLES
by Gonzalo Jover & Emilio G. del Castillo
(1908)

CHARACTERS

Graziella
Betsy Weimer
Raffles
Williams
Sherlock Holmes
Gibolette
Jacob
Gibson
Inspector Hamilton
Max (A Policeman)
Mr. Weimer
1st Man
2nd Man

SCENE I

A Cellar. There is a door on one side. At the rear, there is a large chest.

GRAZIELLA(entering, making sure she's alone): No-body. I can give the signal.
(goes to lattice and sings)

Bird without a nest,
Prowling its cage,
Avoid your chains.
Come, it's your equal who tells you, poor bird.
No one lurks to dethrone you.
(she hums)
RAFFLES (after a moment):
Sad,
To lose liberty,
Seek consolation in the shadows,
And flee the light.
Day frightens.
And alone the dear thing
Comes.
GRAZIELLA:
Bird without nest
Enter without fear.
(she hums)
RAFFLES (spoken as he enters): Graziella says it's safe to come in. Enter, Williams.

WILLIAMS: I'm not confidant. This cursed Holmes has sworn to put his claw on you; it's not very healthy to be around you.

GRAZIELLA: We are alone in the cellar.

WILLIAMS: Have you inspected carefully? The great detective is capable of hiding himself in your own clothes. It would be wise to finish with him once and for all.

RAFFLES: Usually, I abhor violence—but today...

WILLIAMS: You understand what makes it indispensable?

RAFFLES: Being on the point of being in the clutches of my enemy. If it weren't for Graziella—but the magnificent business that was planned, failed. And those are two strokes lost.

WILLIAMS: That's not the worst reason. Gibolette was caught and would—but for your generous help—still be in prison.

GRAZIELLA (to Raffles): You got them out?

RAFFLES: It was my duty.

GRAZIELLA (to Raffles): Ill done, they are both scoundrels!

WILLIAMS: It was a dangerous and audacious escape.

RAFFLES: The important thing is you are here.

WILLIAMS: And afterwards prepared to give new strikes.

GRAZIELLA: All fail. Holmes is watching us. To attempt new adventures is to insist on falling into his clutches. We are in England, Raffles. You will be almost rich, ingenious and powerful.

RAFFLES: It's too soon for me to pull out. Holmes doesn't frighten me. For me to win my bet with him, and to realize my desires requires risk. Against the fortune of Lady Betsy, the daughter of Lord Weimer—I have a powerful recourse.

WILLIAMS: Her complicity to rob her father?

RAFFLES: No. A compromising letter that Lady Betsy wrote me in a fury of passion. What wouldn't either the father or daughter give to redeem this proof of the love of an aristocratic damsel for a famous bandit?

GRAZIELLA: Raffles—this way—

RAFFLES: Is a bit delicate, right? But all's fair in love and war.

WILLIAMS: After all, it's less compromising than a knifing—also less practical.

47

RAFFLES: The practical thing is to be on guard. Holmes knows about this hideout. At any moment he could come to examine it.

WILLIAMS: If he comes alone—

RAFFLES: He'll come alone. Our challenge is man to man.

WILLIAMS: If he enters, he won't leave. I swear it.

RAFFLES: If Holmes enters and leaves, it doesn't matter to me. All that interests me here is that you not recoil, and I'm going to take it with me.

GRAZIELLA: The letter.

RAFFLES: This is it.

(He pulls out a letter.)

GRAZIELLA: From this woman, Raffles. You've deceived me. You love her.

RAFFLES: I only love you, my Graziella. Although I have the presentiment that you will be the cause of my ruin and my death.

GRAZIELLA: I would give my life for you. Don't worry.

RAFFLES (fondly): My Graziella.

WILLIAMS: Now is not the time to coo, my turtledoves. You don't have the letter you need to escape from Police examination. Then, let's go.

RAFFLES: Are you afraid?

WILLIAMS: Afraid? I, Williams? (in a threatening tone) If someone else said that...

RAFFLES: If you want to prove your valor, wait for Holmes here and entertain him.

WILLIAMS: It would be easier to kill him.

RAFFLES: It's enough to entertain him. I will return with reinforcements if we succeed in trapping him in this cellar with no other exit than this door—easy to guard.

Perhaps we will realize the best imaginable business: to make our persecutor our accomplice.

GRAZIELLA: Holmes won't compromise.

RAFFLES: We will impose this condition to spare his life.

WILLIAMS: If Holmes would come over to our side, we would be masters of all the gold in England. But it is impossible.

RAFFLES: Impossible! That word ought not to be in our dictionary. There is nothing impossible to the Will. Graziella, run find Jacob. I'll take care of Gibolette; within fifteen minutes we will meet here again. If Holmes comes before that you know what you must do, Williams: entertain him.

WILLIAMS: That's my account.

RAFFLES: Holmes is an obstacle to our plans.

WILLIAMS: Let me eliminate him.

RAFFLES: Let's go, Graziella.

(Graziella and Raffles leave.)

WILLIAMS: Holmes, come here. We will meet face to face, meet alone. Bah! Audacious as he may be, he knows me, and he wouldn't dare that much.

HOLMES (enters calmly, smoking his pipe. Ironic.): Good evening, friend Williams.

WILLIAMS: Holmes!

HOLMES: Knowing that you would be alone, I came so you wouldn't be bored. I saw Raffles leave, but I imagine he'll be back. Let's wait for him together.

WILLIAMS: It suits me—to spare him disgust.

HOLMES: You're not very polite. The sight of me would disgust him, eh?

WILLIAMS: It does.

HOLMES: Let's find a reason. In short, you avoid it.

WILLIAMS: Me?

49

HOLMES: I only came to propose to you a small business.

WILLIAMS: Let's see.

HOLMES: Raffles has a letter I'm interested in possessing.

WILLIAMS: From Lady Betsy de Weimer.

HOLMES: Exactly. Her honor is in your hands. Give me the letter and get it over with.

WILLIAMS: And what will you give me in exchange?

HOLMES: Fifteen days leave from the prison from which you escaped.

WILLIAMS: That doesn't suit me.

HOLMES: Then you will be captured this very night.

WILLIAMS (incredulous): By you?

HOLMES (firmly): By me.

WILLIAMS: Only if I were disabled.

(Putting his hand in his jacket. Holmes pulls out a pistol and points it at him.)

WILLIAMS (putting up his hands): Now don't go thinking that—

HOLMES: I'm thinking nothing. Produce that letter.

WILLIAMS: I can do that. I have it.

HOLMES: Right. In the inside pocket on the left side of your vest.

WILLIAMS: You know everything.

HOLMES: Everything. Like that sailor.

WILLIAMS (darkly): That was you?

HOLMES: Just the letter.

WILLIAMS: Raffles entrusted it to me. I'm going to give it to you.

(again reaching into his pocket)

HOLMES (warning him): Stay put.

WILLIAMS: But if I am to give it to you—?

HOLMES: Don't move your hands or I shoot.

WILLIAMS: I swear that—

HOLMES: What have you got there? Let's have a look. Keep your hands where I can see them, and be quiet, because I am very nervous and your least movement may cause me to pull the trigger. That would be a shame because this gun is pointed at your heart.

(Holmes searches him with one hand and points his revolver at him with the other.)

HOLMES: Let's go. Here's the letter. The Devil—it's heavier than I thought. Do you know that Miss Betsy uses an unusual sort of paper?

WILLIAMS (planning to recover his revolver): Oh!

HOLMES: Quiet! I'm watching the game— (searching in every pocket of his overcoat) I'm concerned that you have no other, because there's nothing more in this purse. Now, let's talk plainly. You stole this letter from Raffles?

WILLIAMS: Um—I don't know.

HOLMES: A week of leave—if you tell the truth!

WILLIAMS: If that's so—I think—

(He vacillates and then comes to a decision.)

WILLIAMS: After all, you are right. I'm a suspicious brute. Above all, it suits me not to cheat. To be your friend.

HOLMES: I'd like nothing better.

WILLIAMS: And will you trust me?

HOLMES: You shall see. Take your revolver, I'll keep mine. Where is the letter?

WILLIAMS: In some chest or safe.

HOLMES: Better in hand it seems to me.

WILLIAMS: In that chest. (pointing) Take a look and you will find it.

HOLMES: We're going to see. (searching the chest) The chest is empty. You tricked me, Williams.

WILLIAMSL Like you in cleverness.

HOLMES: That will cost you your life.

WILLIAMS: First, you'll lose yours. Like this.

(Pulls the revolver and tries to fire, but nothing happens.)

HOLMES: You are an incredible moron. Did you think I was going to give you this toy back without taking precautions? Fire! Fire! If it diverts you. All the chambers are empty like the chest and when you get tired of it, I will begin. This one is loaded.

WILLIAMS: Oh. I am lost! This man is a demon!

HOLMES: Long live the rat who wanted to play the cat!

RAFFLES (rushing in and taking Holmes' gun): This rat has a tiger's claws!

HOLMES: Raffles!

RAFFLES: Now I'm the strongest. Take your revenge, Williams!

JACOB: And I, mine. I want to avenge myself for having me thrown in the Thames.

GIBOLETTE: I am appreciative of the time spent in prison.

(making similar contortions)

WILLIAMS: Damn! Damn, this weapon!

GRAZIELLA (taking possession the revolver from the hands of Williams): No—a murder, no.

RAFFLES: Graziella!

GRAZIELLA: It would be gallows for you. Cursed weapon.

WILLIAMS: What are you doing? Give it back!

(wrestling the gun from her)

GIBOLETTE: Brother Williams—gallantry with the ladies.

JACOB: Stop the fighting.

GIBOLETTE: I agree.

HOLMES: But what do you want? This woman saved you.

GIBOLETTE: She did? How's that?

HOLMES: My people are on guard here. If you even dream of a shot, they will apprehend you.

GIBOLETTE: We'll be apprehended, too, if Mr. Holmes leaves.

RAFFLES: We won't settle for that.

HOLMES: No?

RAFFLES: No—not without conditions?

HOLMES: I will impose one. Hand over Betsy's letters!

RAFFLES: Are you strange. A prisoner imposes conditions on his warders. Now I am the one who will impose conditions.

HOLMES: Are you going to give me those letters?

GRAZIELLA: Give them up, Raffles. You are heading to disgrace.

GIBOLETTE (aside to Raffles): I would give them to him, maestro.

RAFFLES: Me, no. It's a guaranty and a pass key.

(goes to the door and locks it with the key which he keeps)

RAFFLES: Holmes, this cellar has no other door but the one which I locked. And I'm keeping the key to it.

HOLMES (looking at the lattice): In this lattice there's a need for iron windows.

RAFFLES: You cannot escape from here. Lock and guard this window, Williams.

(Williams goes to the lattice.)

HOLMES: Still, there's a skylight.

RAFFLES: Thirty feet high. I defy you to get to it.

JACOB: You are precise. I put a sentry there.

HOLMES: And what's this all about?

RAFFLES: To tell you that you are in our power, and that you won't get out of here without capitulating. Either you become our associate, or you will become our victim! Choose!

HOLMES: I've decided. I'm leaving without deliberating.

GRAZIELLA: That's impossible.

HOLMES: When I please.

(folds his hands and sits down)

RAFFLES: Try it if you can.

HOLMES: Later. Before that, listen to me attentively. Williams will be taken tonight, and once in power of the court, is a dead man. Gibolette will be taken tomorrow morning, when I've finished using him to defeat you. Raffles, if you don't deliver to me right now the letter I came to get—this is a matter of honor, not a police negotiation. Decide! I give you a moment to think about it.

JACOB: Within a minute you will be a dead man. Take it, Williams.

(gives him a knife and pulls out another)

WILLIAMS: Thanks, Jacob, it will save my neck.

GIBOLETTE: It will be an honor to operate on a famous man.

HOLMES: Let's get this over with, Raffles. The letters, yes or no?

RAFFLES: No.

HOLMES: If I leave without them, you'll be sorry.

RAFFLES: Are you certain of leaving?

HOLMES: I think so.

WILLIAMS: When and how?

HOLMES: Now—and like this.

(Rapidly he overturns the seat in which he was leaning. The lamp breaks and goes out. The stage is absolutely dark.)

JACOB: Get him, Williams!

WILLIAMS: Ah, Satan, bring him within my reach!

JACOB: Cursed detective!

GIBOLETTE: I got him.

JACOB: That's me, you idiot!

RAFFLES: Shut up! Everybody be quiet. He cannot escape.

GRAZIELLA: Lights! Lights!

RAFFLES: The window. Open the window!

GRAZIELLA: The window! Light! Open it, Williams!

WILLIAMS(opens the window and a ray of light shines in): There it is!

JACOB: Now, we'll get you!

RAFFLES: Holmes! Where's he?

GRAZIELLA: Gone!

RAFFLES: Gone! But there's no exit!

JACOB: The Devil's in it! He's escaped! But—where'd he go?

GIBOLETTE: The trap door is open.

(pointing to an open trap door.)

WILLIAMS: The skylight.

RAFFLES: It's impossible to scale it.

JACOB: He's down there.

GIBOLETTE: Better. No one will hear his screams. That's where the body will stay.

GRAZIELLA: Don't kill him! Don't kill him!

WILLIAMS: Shut up! Everyone into the cellar!

(Raffles, Jacob, Williams and Gibolette go into the subcellar.)

GRAZIELLA: Gone to shed blood! My beloved Raffles will be a murderer! Impossible! (to the sub-cellar) Raffles! Raffles! Don't kill him. For God's sake, don't kill him.

HOLMES (emerging from behind the chest): My thanks for your good wishes.

GRAZIELLA: You!

HOLMES: I'll try to repay you. Though it will benefit Raffles.

GRAZIELLA (with dread): Get out quickly. Go back the way you came. Through this door.

(she goes to open it)

GRAZIELLA: O My God! It's locked. And Raffles kept the key.

HOLMES: Don't take the trouble of worrying how to open for me. I have a skeleton key.

(Taking out a key and opening the door)

GRAZIELLA: They're coming back up! Run! I will ask the Virgin to help you.

HOLMES: That's the thing. You talk to the Virgin—I'll run. And the miracle of saving myself is complete. Convey my apologies to Raffles. Tell him I'm didn't have the time to wait.

C U R T A I N

SCENE II

A Street. Gibson runs in followed by several men trying to catch him.

1st MAN: Catch him! Catch him!

GIBSON: Lemme go! I haven't done anything special.

OTHERS: He's a thief.

GIBSON: That's a slander. And it greatly injures my reputation.

1st MAN: He robbed a gentleman of his scarf and watch.

GIBSON: I'm not a robber. I'm a singer and a dancer.

2nd MAN: Yes or no? Should we hand him over to the Police?

3rd MAN: Let's give him a beating and let him go in peace.

1st MAN: You're going to get it.

GIBSON: We'll see about that.

(He stands like a boxer but when the men approach him he takes to his heels.)

GIBSON: Help! Help! You'll never catch me.

(He eludes them, but they still pursue him.)

GRAZIELLA (entering): What screams! Gibson!? (to the men) Why are you chasing him?

2nd MAN: He's a robber, a thief.

GRAZIELLA: You are mistaken, gentlemen—this kid is—

1st MAN: What is he?

GRAZIELLA: He's my brother. He's naughty, but not bad.

2nd MAN: Leave him in peace. Goodnight.

(The men pursuing Gibson leave.)

GRAZIELLA: You are incorrigible. You promised me to stop.

GIBSON: I did stop. Only this toff put his watch under my nose. It was gold. Then he pulled out this silk handkerchief. That was too much. You see what temptation does.

GRAZIELLA: Gibson—you are young. Use a bit of willpower and give up this life which continues to bring you down. You know that Holmes, the famous detective will protect you.

GIBSON: Do I know it? It's certain I serve him. And now I see I've done a favor to the toffs.

GRAZIELLA: You?

GIBSON: Profiting by the negligence of Raffles; he left the letter of Lady Betsy.

GRAZIELLA: You've got it?

GIBSON: Have a look.

GRAZIELLA: If Raffles were to guess!

GIBSON: That doesn't scare me. Having advised Lady Betsy to come get the letter in this place, I also told Mr. Holmes.

GRAZIELLA: What did she say to Raffles in this letter? Did she talk to him of his sweetness? Does he reply to others as sweetly as he does to me? I am curious.

GIBSON: Would you like to read it?

GRAZIELLA: And if this letter reveals that Raffles truly loves her?

GIBSON: Let's get rid of doubts. Don't be stupid.
(He opens the letter.)

GRAZIELLA: Go, woman. If all are curious and none know what to do. Listen.

GIBSON (reading): "My love—hope of my life..."

GRAZIELLA: Shut up! Can't you see jealousy has entered my heart?

GIBSON: "Without you, all is sad in my soul..."

GRAZIELLA: She doesn't know that sorrow is the faithful and inseparable companion of all tender love.

GIBSON: "Only memory animates my sadness. Only my memory of your ardent caresses..."

GRAZIELLA: Don't read any more. The pain is killing me.

GIBSON: "You swore..."

GRAZIELLA: What did you read this letter to me for? Raffles feigns love with so much art—who can tell truth from lies?

HOLMES (entering): Truth is an eternal problem.

GRAZIELLA: Holmes!

HOLMES: I sympathize with you. The greatest beauty of life is bitter. And makes you sad.

GIBSON: You are very good, Mr. Holmes, and I'm very happy to be able to demonstrate my gratitude with action.

HOLMES: What have you done, kid?

GIBSON: Taken Lady Betsy's letter from Raffles.

HOLMES: Are you sure?

GIBSON: Absolutely sure. I have it here.

(pointing to the letter)

HOLMES: How did you learn where Raffles kept it?

GIBSON: Because he doesn't suspect me, he put it in a purse in my presence.

HOLMES: In a purse where you could put your hand? Go on, go on. I understand nothing about Raffles, if you confide your ability to me.

GIBSON: Mr. Holmes...

HOLMES: Raffles suspects that you are in an understanding with me, and that you would steal it.

GIBSON: I don't understand.

HOLMES: Would there were exact proof of its authenticity. Let's have a look. Who has made so many folds in this paper?

GIBSON: He did it so he'd recognize it in his hands.

HOLMES: That's it. So many enter in his abandoned office—and on the table; a small chest with so many of his jewels. No one watches because all think that shortly the owner is leaving clandestinely so as not to be surprised in a meeting with me. Well planned.

GRAZIELLA: And what would this lady care about losing her jewels—compared to losing her reputation ? It's worth more. And what about the letter?

HOLMES: In your place you wouldn't be jealous of her.

GRAZIELLA: You are so expressive.

HOLMES: This one—what about the other?

GRAZIELLA: What! There's another! Another letter—I read it.

HOLMES (seeing Betsy): Silence! She's coming.

GIBSON (to Betsy): Here you have Mr. Holmes.

HOLMES: At your service!

BETSY: And the letter?

HOLMES: Read it without getting emotional—

BETSY(taking it): Thank you. You've saved my reputation.

GRAZIELLA: By hiding the guilt.

BETSY: What did you say?

GRAZIELLA: Raffles got you hot—without much trouble it seems.

BETSY: That reproach is unfair. Raffles made so many protestations to me that I believed in his love. But without giving myself to him. This letter proves it.

GRAZIELLA: This letter proves the contrary.

BETSY: It would show you so.

GRAZIELLA (opens the letter and reads it): "My love—the hope of my life..."

BETSY: I never wrote that.

GIBSON: Then I wrote it.

HOLMES: The letter is false. I'm sure of that.

BETSY: But what about the real one?

HOLMES: Still in Raffles power.

GRAZIELLA: Will you swear to me that you didn't write this?

BETSY: I swear it.

GRAZIELLA: Then I swear to you that this very night you will have the real one back. Even if it must be torn from the power of Raffles.

HOLMES: Get his letter tonight, and tonight Raffles will be caught. What's more urgent is that you get back to your house, accompanied by Gibson—before going to Finchley tunnel.

GIBSON: Near the mysterious lair of Raffles.

HOLMES: The nearest possible. Others watch there—and give him a signal that this young lady is not in her home. He will suppose that she's searching to take her letter from him, and that will be useful by giving him the time needed to steal your jewels.

BETSY: I don't care if he takes them.

GIBSON: Shall we go, Miss?

BETSY: Yes—but alone! This affair is so unforeseeable.

HOLMES: Don't be afraid. Raffles is taking great care not to alarm you because he's confident that you won't report the robbery of your jewels—so he won't publicize the story of your relationship.

BETSY: If I wasn't dealing with a bandit, I would have no interest in hiding it.

GRAZIELLA: I offer it so as to recover your belongings.

BETSY: Let's go there.

GIBSON(aside): Always nice to spend time with a woman by the light of the moon. Decidedly, I am lucky. (leaving with Betsy)

HOLMES: How long do you think it will take you to get this paper?

GRAZIELLA: An hour.

HOLMES: Where will we meet?

GRAZIELLA: In the Finchley esplanade—near the tunnel.

HOLMES: I'll go now.

GRAZIELLA: Your word?

HOLMES: Word of Holmes—and that's more than a word of honor!

C U R T A I N

SCENE III

The same as Scene III with Holmes and Raffles.
Moonlight.

WILLIAMS: This is the place. I know the house very well.
GIBOLETTE: Right. I've been in it. It's not stupid.
WILLIAMS: Be careful what you say.
GIBOLETTE: The father works in the office. You can see the light from the garden—through the blinds.
WILLIAMS(seemingly impatient): Eh?
GIBOLETTE: What's going on?
WILLIAMS: Don't you hear anything?
GIBOLETTE: What?
WILLIAMS: Like people breathing nearby.
GIBOLETTE: There's nothing. Here is the jewel box. And it's loaded.
WILLIAMS: Be alert. I am not easy.
GIBOLETTE(a cry): Ah!
WILLIAMS: What?
GIBOLETTE: That curtain. I think it moved.
WILLIAMS: It must be the breeze.
GIBOLETTE: Before you thought you heard breathing, Could it be an ambush?
WILLIAMS: Look! Jewels on the table.
GIBOLETTE: So much booty.
(looking around)
WILLIAMS: Gold. Diamonds. Excellent take!
HAMILTON(emerging from behind the curtain with other police): Quite excellent. In the end, you fell for it, jailbirds!

WILLIAMS and GIBOLETTE: Ah!

HAMILTON: And with the corpus delicti. Are you well caught! Only Sherlock Holmes prepares things this way.

WILLIAMS: Treachery! Raffles has betrayed us.

GIBOLETTE: Only he knew of the planned robbery.

HAMILTON: In the name of the law—

GIBOLETTE: The window! The garden! Let's flee!

WILLIAMS (knife in hand): I pass no matter what!

HAMILTON: There's no escape. My men are planted everywhere.

POLICEMAN (pulling a revolver): Surrender or I shoot.

WILLIAMS: Who cares! One must die one way or another. I'm passing.

RAFFLES (entering, dressed as a cop, grabbing the two bandits): Pipe down, swine!

HAMILTON: Bravo, companion!

RAFFLES: Order of detective Sherlock Holmes. Raffles is in this case. You must detain him. Search everywhere. I'll take care of these characters.

HAMILTON: Raffles! Here, Max, I have the keys. (to Raffles) Don't let these any of these bandits escape, companion.

RAFFLES: I'll answer for them. Gibolette's a strangler, and Williams a murderer. I know their worth. Be calm.

HAMILTON: Let's go! This is going to be the best police business of my life.

(Hamilton and the Policeman leave.)

WILLIAMS: We fall in the end into his clutches.

GIBOLETTE (darkly): Raffles!

RAFFLES: Silence! Climb down into the garden. I've sent the police on a false scent. Let's take advantage of the time.

WILLIAMS: And the loot?

GIBOLETTE: Wait for us in the cellar to divide the loot. Fast. Someone's coming.

WILLIAMS: Let's go.

VOICES: The burglars! Help!

RAFFLES: Now it's my turn. Here's the jewel box. Take the jewels.

(He opens the bag of loot and finds the false arm he left Holmes with in the previous play.) The clutches of Holmes. I begin to think I am lost.

HAMILTON: This way!

POLICEMAN: Here are the two thieves.

SHOUTS: Get them! Get them!

WEIMER: But what about Raffles? What about Raffles?

RAFFLES: He was just here. He snatched my prisoners. All three fled. After them. Help me. Ah, I see them! Halt in the name of the law!

(Raffles leaves running.)

HAMILTON: You are a fine companion. But get going, Max. Run to help him.

(They leave.)

WEIMER: What's this? The jewel box is empty. The theft has been committed. This man must be another bandit disguised as a policeman. Help!

(He rushes after them.)

(Yelling in the distance. Holmes enters imperturbably, smoking his pipe.)

HOLMES: The jewels are here.

(emptying the bag of loot.)

HOLMES: All they got were some cheap costume jewelry.

WEIMER: Oh, thank you, Mr. Holmes!

CURTAIN

SCENE IV

Williams and Gibolette come running in.

WILLIAMS: Good run. I think they cannot catch us.

GIBOLETTE: They lost the trail.

WILLIAMS: Are you sure?

GIBOLETTE: We ran the most scared in our lives.

WILLIAMS: Holmes has sworn to catch us tonight.

GIBOLETTE: All he's done is to prevent us from living peacefully.

WILLIAMS: What?

GIBOLETTE: My admiration for Raffles doesn't go to the point of sacrificing my tranquility.

WILLIAMS: That's it. Suppressing Raffles we would change to good times. Holmes would be grateful to us.

GIBOLETTE: We'd be hanging ourselves.

WILLIAMS: You think?

GIBOLETTE: The best thing would be for an accident—well prepared. You understand. Your knife's already marked.

WILLIAMS: An accident. I don't see how—

GIBOLETTE: For example. Push him in front of a train.

WILLIAMS: He would jump—no matter where we pushed him.

GIBOLETTE: If he were tied up, no.

WILLIAMS: True. But the ropes would denounce the crime. Bye, bye, accident.

GIBOLETTE: I appreciate that. But, still—no one would suspect that you—so famously attached to your knife-- would change your modus operandi to rid yourself of a companion in adventures. You, especially are more quick—

WILLIAMS: It would be safer. The blade goes to the heart nobly. It's just a stroke, a blow, a hoarse cry. And it's all over. But what makes you think that the other is safer? The engineer sees the body and stops the train. Raffles escapes, and—we receive a just reward.

GIBOLETTE: Placing him by the exit from the tunnel, the engineer won't be able to see him. No one will come. There's no time to control the train, and halt the train.

WILLIAMS: Precisely. The train is moving with precaution through the tunnel.

GIBOLETTE: To do this we must leave him at the mouth of the tunnel; then enter inside the tunnel, climb on the train, place ourselves in a place sheltered by shadows, after that we get out at Watford which is the first stopping point. There we rid ourselves of the jewels, and with the money we secure, proceed to Midland!

WILLIAMS: What then?

GIBOLETTE: Go to India. Wherever we go, we will live by our wits and our agile hands.

WILLIAMS: So long as it's far from Holmes.

GIBOLETTE: Our skin will be much safer.

WILLIAMS: Notwithstanding, we are known to the police. Until we get out of England it would be prudent to travel separately. A person alone deceives vigilance. It's the defect of accomplices.

GIBOLETTE: We will separate at Watford, if you like. (aside) You won't get to Watford.

WILLIAMS: We shall see. If I decide the plan doesn't suit me. I have more confidence in the strength of my arm.

GIBOLETTE: Come to the esplanade, we'll discuss it on the way. Raffles will wait in the city, and it's here we'll wait carrying the treasure he doesn't know escaped from the bag.

WILLIAMS: A fortune. Happiness for a single person.

GIBOLETTE: Oh, but there are three of us.

WILLIAMS: Oh, three, three.

GIBOLETTE: If we suppress Raffles it will be two.

WILLIAMS: Fine, we'll make it two. (aside) For now. Before leaving for Watford.

GIBOLETTE: We'll each have enough. I'm not ambitious.

WILLIAMS: No. Better to have a dozen books than a bad sale.

GIBOLETTE: Twelve thousand. Maybe double that. Let's go to the Esplanade. You go first.

(seeing Williams fingering his knife)

WILLIAMS: As you like. (aside) Little remaining time for him.

(he leaves)

GIBOLETTE (aside): Before leaving for Watford. (gripping his cord for strangling)

(The two leave.)

GIBSON (who's been eavesdropping): Each of them is thinking of killing each other, and both of killing Raffles. Raffles knows that I'm treating with Holmes. To collect my share. Yeah. I will avoid it—because I still have a bit of fondness. Bad to dress badly—but without skin one is more cold than without clothes. In winter it's rough, and I must have shelter, lots of shelter. To assure the arms of Graziella will shelter me, I laugh like spring.

GRAZIELLA (entering): Gibson.

GIBSON: Come. I was just thinking about you. Actually, I'm always thinking of you.

GRAZIELLA: Bad things?

GIBSON: Don't believe that—it would be very wrong. But you only think about Raffles.

68

GRAZIELLA: I just saw him. He thinks that I took the letter.

GIBSON: And how did you do it?

GRAZIELLA: I employed supplications and threats. With the result that—he understood. Necessarily, he convinced me that my jealousy had no reason. It would have driven me crazy with suspicion.

GIBSON: How you love him!

GRAZIELLA: The way I abhor him.

GIBSON: You?

GRAZIELLA: My passion is very odd. But we won't speak of it. You must advise Holmes that the letter is in my power.

GIBSON: I'll run to tell him. But don't rest. Go to the Esplanade tunnel in Finchley Road. Raffles is in danger.

GRAZIELLA: What are you saying?

GIBSON: You cause me pain, Graziella. Williams and Gibolette are plotting to rid themselves of your lover. This very night. Perhaps in a short while—in the Esplanade.

GRAZIELLA: In the Esplanade. My Raffles—My God—How—?

(She leaves.)

GIBSON: And now, I inform Sherlock Holmes.

(He leaves hurriedly.)

CURTAIN

SCENE V

The Mouth of the tunnel in Finchley Road. Night.

GIBOLETTE: Are we agreed?

WILLIAMS: We are.

GIBOLETTE: Then let's examine the terrain to prepare ourselves.

WILLIAMS: Suppose he stays in London?

GIBOLETTE: He won't fail. Besides, this is the road the poor take against all persecution.

WILLIAMS: But as Holmes knows about it, it will be abandoned as insecure.

GIBOLETTE: Enough—we don't have time. Let's go into the tunnel to select the site where we will make the train jump. Did you bring a lantern?

WILLIAMS: Yes.

GIBOLETTE: Then let's go in.

(They go in. A short pause.)

GRAZIELLA: Nothing. I've wasted time. Before, they were not suspicious. What's that? Could it be him? Raffles! Raffles!

BETSY (starting): Where is Raffles?

GRAZIELLA: Have you come in search of him?

BETSY: Yes. My house was broken into. He's being pursued everywhere.

GRAZIELLA: And you pretend to save him?

BETSY: I pretend that it's not in the power of Justice to hold the proof of my love.

GRAZIELLA: Nothing more than that?

BETSY: I committed the folly of coming only to get that letter.

GRAZIELLA: You shall have it—trust in me.

BETSY: Thank you, my friend.

GRAZIELLA: As of today, I'm your best friend—Graziella, the Neapolitan. (seeing Betsy intends to leave) Are you leaving?

BETSY: Yes. They don't know in my house that I went out.

GRAZIELLA: I'll go part of the way with you. This place is very dangerous.

(They leave together.)

WILLIAMS: Did you hear? They are looking for Raffles everywhere.

GIBOLETTE: Silence!

WILLIAMS: It's Raffles!

(They retreat into the tunnel.)

RAFFLES (entering, worried): The clutches of Sherlock Holmes. I won't let him catch me. He knows how to trick me. Another stroke failed. When I worked alone, I never lacked anything. Gibolette and Williams are two fools that compromise my work. From now on, I don't want to do anything in their company.

GIBOLETTE (to Williams, emerging from the tunnel): Now!

WILLIAMS: Yes.

(They hurl themselves on Raffles, subdue him and tie him up.)

RAFFLES: Ah, bandits, wretches!

GIBOLETTE: The mouth. Compliments don't please me.

RAFFLES: Release me, cowards!

GIBOLETTE: A gag. Like this.

(gagging Raffles)

WILLIAMS: The bale is made. On our way.

GIBOLETTE: And to the preparation.

(They place Raffles on the track.)

WILLIAMS: That's it. You cannot move the guilty. (to Raffles) Don't be afraid. The train moves very rapidly and you won't suffer much. But what about the loot? Did you bring the contents of the bags? (looking) Nothing. Not one jewel. The rogue swindled us.

GIBOLETTE: Might the jewels be in the cellar? Perhaps, before coming, he left them?

WILLIAMS: We've seen enough of him

(Train whistle)

GIBOLETTE: Do you hear?

WILLIAMS: The train.

GIBOLETTE: I wouldn't give him the way out.

WILLIAMS: Let's go to the cellar.

(Pause. Raffles lies on the track. The noise of the train increases and approaches. Holmes appears.)

HOLMES (running in): There's no time! Stop! Stop!

(He fires at the train in the tunnel. The whistle gets louder. Graziella rushes in and throws herself over Raffles, mad with tears.)

GRAZIELLA: Raffles! Raffles! (to Holmes) Holmes! The letter for his life.

HOLMES: Give me the letter. The honor of Lady Betsy is saved.

RAFFLES (untied by Graziella): I'm vanquished. You win the bet.

(Gibolette and Williams enter led by Hamilton and Police. Gibson comes with them.)

HOLMES: Give it to the poor of London, with other thousands in my purse.

RAFFLES: You can be proud of your triumph.

HOLMES: Not this way. Without being face to face, heart to heart—as I wanted to give you—the clutches of Sherlock Holmes.

(Graziella hugs Raffles. The train is almost emerging from the tunnel

As the curtain falls.)

CURTAIN

THE TRIUMPH OF FANTÔMAS

by Jose Maria Martin de Eugenio
(1915)

CHARACTERS

Sister Teresa
Princess Lionelle
The Marquise de Grantley
The Duchess de Guerin
Ruy (a police officer)
Mr. Juez (Police Commissioner)
Mr. Verdier (his clerk)
The Doctor
Leopold
The Duke de Guerin
Inspector Juve
Gamer (a Minister)
Lamerit (another Minister)
Sir Edeval (Minister of Justice)
The Marquis de Grantley
A Pierrot
A Harlequin
M. Maurier
Ladies, Gentlemen, Masked Fantômases, Masks.

The action takes place in London in 1912.

ACT I

The Palace of the Duke de Guerin. A magnificent room. There is a large fireplace with a bust of a famous English personality on the mantelpiece, and a desk with its back to a balcony. On the floor, near the desk, is a man's body covered with a sheet or a blanket. Electric lights. A central light and a table lamp. Doors on all sides.

AT RISE, Ruy, a police officer is speaking to Sister Teresa, a Sister of Mercy.

RUY: What is your opinion of this extraordinary case, Sister Teresa? This rich and noble gentleman, completely happy, it appears, in love with his young and beautiful wife, shuts himself in here—as is natural to write letters, smoke—between the heat and humidity weighing on him, he got up calmly to open this balcony. He opens it, breathes a little, then returns to his table to continue writing, but—never got there. Death surprised him, he tumbled down there without even saying, hey, I'm dying.

SISTER TERESA: Poor man.

RUY: His wife, puzzled by his being late, waits a while, screams, turning to a manservant, the only one they had in the house—the rest goes down quickly—the servant comes running to tell you; then he called us by telephone; we came; my companion goes in search of Juez, and the Commissioner, and here we are, you and I, keeping vigil over this poor gentleman...

SISTER TERESA: Fatality, friend Ruy, fatality.

RUY: Indubitably, the gentleman suffered an aneurism whose rupture occasioned his death.

SISTER TERESA: Who knows?

RUY: The lady has shut herself up in her rooms—and wants to see no one until Juez comes.

SISTER TERESA: Poor lady!

RUY: And I, in all honesty, cannot keep myself from being hungry and sleepy.

SISTER TERESA: I'm not hungry, but sleepy, yes. The previous night was spent in a vigil at Count d'Arley's near here.

RUY: Another accident, little sister, that makes your hair stand on end. I believe that Juve, the great detective, is hot on the scent of some terrible crime, don't you know?

SISTER TERESA: He came immediately and took charge of the situation.

RUY: I will learn from him. He's the king of detectives.

SISTER TERESA: God keep him!

(Pause.)

RUY: Do you allow me, little sister, to go wet my whistle? I'll bring some for you if you like.

SISTER TERESA: I cannot drink anything, but you go.

RUY: Mr. Juez the Police Commissioner is late enough.

SISTER TERESA: I believe it. You go—don't worry and drink as much as you please. Put out this central light and light this other one on the table. This one, with its red screen already lights the dwelling in an agreeable semi-darkness.

RUY(pointing to the body): This doesn't scare you?

SISTER TERESA: Me? I've seen so many in this situation that—God forgive me, I look on it with indifference.

RUY(going): I'll be back right away.

(He leaves.

(After Ruy goes out, Sister Teresa begins to doze off. A secret door in the chimney opens and Fantômas enters furtively with pistol drawn. Seeing that Teresa is asleep

and no one in the room, he gestures and two more individuals emerge from the chimney-door, both dressed as
Fantômas.

(While they carry in the body of a woman, place it where
the man's body was, Fantômas goes to the balcony and
closes it,

(Meanwhile the two masked men remove the man's
body. Fantômas never takes his eyes off Sister Teresa
and the door.

(Once the exchange of bodies is complete, he returns the
way he came and shuts the secret door behind him, silently. All this is performed silently and with great effi-
ciency.)

SISTER TERESA: Oof! What a stifling heat. Huh?
(going to balcony window)

SISTER TERESA: Who closed the balcony? (puzzled)
Are you back, Ruy?

RUY(returning): This way, gentlemen.

(Ruy enters with Mr. Juez, the Police Commissioner, his
clerk, Mr. Verdier, and two policemen who guard the
door.)

RUY (to the Commissioner): If it seems good to you, we
will allow time for the doctor to get here. He will tell us
what killed this gentleman.

JUEZ: Whatever you prefer. But, as before, this cursed
business with Count d'Arley prevents me from living
peacefully.

RUY: What about Inspector Juve?

JUEZ: He already makes my life even worse. What a
man! Tireless! (to the Sister) Hello Sister Teresa, is it
you?

SISTER TERESA: At your service.

JUEZ: Yesterday there, today here. So we meet again.

SISTER TERESA: Would that we meet no more.

JUEZ: You were the first to arrive, right?

SISTER TERESA: And Officer Ruy.

RUY: Present!

JUEZ: Fine. Everything else is here—and no one has entered?

SISTER TERESA: No, no.

JUEZ: The way it looks to me, this poor man died suddenly, perhaps because of an aneurism. Did you know him from before?

SISTER TERESA: Yes, sir. The Duke de Guerin is not unknown to me—especially the Duchess who comes to our chapel with some frequency.

JUEZ: Good people, right?

SISTER TERESA: I cannot say anything to the contrary.

JUEZ: Rich?

SISTER TERESA: To judge by their comfort, their lifestyle, their limousines—yes, sir.

JUEZ: In a short while, the doctor will order the raising of the cadaver—and we are going to open yet another criminal investigation. Holy word! I'm already worn out! Mr. Ruy, inform the Duchess and, after that, the servant.

(Ruy leaves.)

JUEZ: We are going to do things by the book. Go ahead, Mr. Verdier, sit down at this table.

VERDIER: Give me a minute.

(He prepares his writing materials.)

RUY (returning): She's coming right away.

JUEZ: Did you see her?

RUY: No, sir. I gave her the message through the door.

(Leopold enters.)

RUY: Here comes the servant. (to Leopold) Police Commissioner Juez needs you.

LEOPOLD: I am at the orders of Mr. Juez.

JUEZ: I have a few questions. How long have you served the Duke?

LEOPOLD: The De Guerins?

JUEZ: Yes, the De Guerins.

LEOPOLD: Two years.

JUEZ: Bravo. And you got along well?

LEOPOLD: Wonderfully.

JUEZ: Admirable!—We don't need to go into that now, right?

LEOPOLD: No, sir.

JUEZ: Things were good among the other servants?

LEOPOLD: Two angels in the whole world.

JUEZ: Your employer suffered from no chronic infirmities?

LEOPOLD: I don't think so.

JUEZ: Fine. The forensic examiner will remove all doubts.

RUY: Here he comes.

(The Doctor enters escorted by a police officer.)

JUEZ: Thank God you're here.

DOCTOR: Pardon, pardon all of you, but the duties of my workload...

JUEZ: You're pardoned, Doctor. Be so good as to inspect this cadaver right away.

DOCTOR: Immediately.

(After taking off his hat and gloves, he kneels down, raising the sheet covering the head of the cadaver, and says in a natural tone)

DOCTOR: What a beautiful woman.

ALL: Huh???

DOCTOR: I said she's a very beautiful woman.

SISTER TERESA: Jesus!

JUEZ: What did he say?

RUY: Look—

80

DOCTOR (completely uncovering the body of a young blonde lady elegantly dressed): I don't know from what this astonishment proceeds. This is the cadaver of a lady killed by a dagger driven into her heart.

(Withdraws and abandons his place to Juez.)

SISTER TERESA: That's impossible!

RUY: This cannot be!

LEOPOLD: We must be dreaming!

JUEZ: One must surrender before the evidence!

DUKE (entering): Good evening, gentlemen.

RUY: The Duke!

LEOPOLDO: My employer!

SISTER TERESA: The Duke de Guerin!

(short pause)

JUEZ: Are you the Duke de Guerin, master of this house?

DUKE: At your service.

JUEZ (to Leopold): Do you recognize your employer?

LEOPOLD: Perfectly.

JUEZ (to Sister Teresa): It's him—him?

SISTER TERESA (unhesitatingly): Yes, sir.

JUEZ (to Ruy): This gentleman is—

RUY: I swear it!

DUKE: What's going on? Is something more going on besides the vile murder of my beloved spouse?

JUEZ: This is stupendous! Milord, would you have the goodness to give me a statement?

DUKE: With great pleasure.

JUEZ: I just want you to answer a few questions. You just said—"the vile murder of my beloved spouse."

DUKE: Exactly.

JUEZ: Tell us about this unhappy situation.

SISTER TERESA, LEOPOLD, RUY (protesting): But...

JUEZ: Silence! Let him speak!

DUKE (with energy): My wife had the habit of writing to her family in Russia every week. Naturally, she came here to my office to do it. This evening she was late returning—very late—and I became worried. So I came here to find her—to meet my poor spouse—the Duchess, as we are at this moment. I heard some horrible shouting. I hurried to find Leopold, whom I ordered to find a Sister of Charity that would aid us, and to telephone the Police—that was done, and the Sister of Charity accompanied by Leopold soon arrived. At that time, worn out by sorrow, I retired to my living quarters. That is all.

JUEZ (to Leopold, Sister Teresa and Ruy): Is all this true?

ALL THREE (with hesitation): No, sir.

DUKE: What—really? What are you saying?

JUEZ: Let's see what occurred. You first, Mr. Leopold.

LEOPOLD: The Duke and the Duchess ate dinner at the usual time. After dinner, they retired to their rooms, A little while later, the Duke came here into his office and began to write letters—for that reason, I withdrew, dismissed the cook, who, with the Duke's permission, went to spend the night with his family. Then, I set to brushing the Duke's clothes, and I heard screams that came from this room—I rushed here and met the Duchess who was a prey to the greatest desperation, and found the Duke stretched there, near you—like so—inanimate, dead. The Duchess ordered me to find a Sister of Charity to help us—in such an unfortunate moment—and she called the Police by telephone. I left and when I returned, Sister Teresa was here, as well as Ruy, and his fellow officers—all waiting for us, with the door already closed. Sister Teresa, Mr. Ruy, isn't this all true?

SISTER TERESA: The exact truth. The Duchess withdrew, weeping, to her rooms, and the gentleman and I remained watching the corpse. Meanwhile, your colleague hurried in search of you.

DUKE: Mr. Juez, there can be no doubt. I'm alive and healthy—unlike my poor wife who—

JUEZ: Let's see. Come here, all of you. Is this the Duchess?

ALL THREE: There's not the slightest doubt.

JUEZ: All three of you are completely crazy!

SISTER TERESA (protesting): Mr. Juez!

JUEZ: Understand, sister, that reality imposes...

SISTER TERESA: Yes, but I—I... (weeping) There's some deep mystery here, Mr. Juez.

RUY: For sure!

JUEZ: Did you leave the corpse?

SISTER TERESA: Not for a moment.

JUEZ: Did anyone enter here?

SISTER TERESA: Absolutely not.

JUEZ: Consequently, the Duke is right and you are...

DOCTOR: Mr. Juez, excuse me for interrupting, but here—in the hand of the victim—she holds a paper. Let's see if I can open her hand... Ah-ha!

(removing paper and handing it to Juez)

DOCTOR: Take it.

JUEZ (examining it): Eh? What's this? What does it mean? A Number 13 with a Question Mark. It's the same card that we found on Count d'Arley. (to Verdier) Mr. Verdier, call the Station and tell them to find the great Inspector Juve, and ask him to come immediately. Let none of those present leave this house. You, Mr. Ruy, find two more officers to station at the door with orders not to allow anyone to leave.

RUY(leaving): In a hurry.

JUEZ: Let's suspend all actions, all business, until the arrival of Inspector Juve—the king of detectives.

(The telephone bell rings.)

JUEZ: Police Commissioner Juez here. Find detective Juve immediately. It's the most serious case. Eh? Very well. They say that Juve's there. He's coming to the phone. (to the telephone) Hello, Mr. Juve. Yes, This is Mr. Juez. I have asked that you be called without losing a minute. Fine. Goodbye. (to the rest) In the next few minutes, we shall have here the one man who can get us out of this imbroglio.

DUKE: Don't you know that gladdens me!

JUEZ: I agree—we all want answers. (to all) Do you all persist in your affirmations?

ALL THREE: We persist.

JUEZ: Think about it carefully.

SISTER TERESA: I swear it before God.

RUY: I swore it once and will a thousand times.

(noise of an auto)

JUEZ: Could that be Juve already?

(All listen.)

JUEZ: He's coming. Yes, he's arriving. He's here.

(Pause. (Juve enters—elegant, shaved, monocled)

JUVE: Quiet everyone. No one has touched anything, right, Mr. Juez?

JUEZ: Nothing. You can work without worrying.

JUVE: That's what I'll do.

(Juve examines the room. Goes to the corpse, then to the balcony and back again.)

JUVE: Without equivocating, what happened here is as follows: this lady, who is the lady of this house, and the wife of this gentleman—

JUEZ: The Duke de Guerin!

JUVE (bows): She was here, where I am standing, when death entered by this balcony—in the shape of an assassin who killed her with a dagger. Is it this one?

84

JUEZ: It appears that way, but...

JUVE: But what?

JUEZ: But Sister Teresa, Leopold, the manservant, and Officer Ruy, all insist that the body which was covered with this sheet was that of the Duke and not that of the Duchess, as we all saw, fully astonished, naturally, when it was uncovered by the Doctor.

JUVE: What are you saying? Did I hear wrong?

JUEZ: You heard perfectly well.

JUVE: Who was watching over the body?

SISTER TERESA: A serving girl.

RUY: And a servant.

JUVE (to the Duke): Milord, what do you say to this?

DUKE: What do expect me to say? I am alive. The body is that of my wife. These people—

JUVE: These people are crazy.

DUKE: I wouldn't go that far.

JUVE (meditating a moment): Mr. Juez, the evidence cannot be dismissed; these people are undoubtedly the victims of a hallucination. We must seek the killer of the Duchess, right, Milord?

DUKE: I'm of the same opinion. I am ready to place at your disposition my entire fortune in order to succeed in finding the assassin.

JUVE (meaningfully): All will be done, Milord.

DUKE: And finally, if he agrees, I will beg Mr. Juez, in light of my rank, title and reputation, to let me take the body of my wife, avoiding the horrible operation of an autopsy on her beloved body.

JUEZ: What's the opinion of Inspector Juve?

JUVE: The Lord Duke is perfectly right. The request seems very natural to me.

JUEZ: Then, no need for more discussion. The Lord Duke can, as of right now, dispose of the body of his unfortunate spouse. Mr. Verdier, draw up the order immediately.

VERDIER: I shall.

JUVE: I have a petition for the Lord Duke.

DUKE: Say it.

JUVE: I want you to allow me to stay in your house for the whole time necessary to clear up these facts.

DUKE: Let it be known that Mr. Juve is absolute lord in this house and can stay for whatever time is necessary.

JUVE: Many and repeated thanks.

JUEZ: Our mission in this house is over for now. Let's be on our way. (to the Duke) Milord, a thousand pardons. I join you in your undeserved sorrow.

DUKE: I remain highly grateful to you, Commissioner.

JUEZ: Mr. Juve, we will return tomorrow at the earliest time.

JUVE: That's fine, sir. I'll await your arrival here. When you get here, have me informed.

JUEZ: Good luck.

JUVE: Don't let Officer Ruy leave—or the others who were watching the body.

JUEZ (to Ruy): You heard him.

(Juez, Verdier and Ruy's officers leave.)

JUVE: You ought to retire, Milord, and get some rest. You go with him, Leopold. Sister Teresa and I will care of the body of your spouse.

DUKE: If that's the way you want it.

JUVE: Yes, I want to be alone to study the subject carefully.

DUKE: Then let's go.

(He goes to the body, kneels and kisses it, weeping.)

JUEZ: Let's go, Milord! Calmness! There's no other remedy.

(He escorts the Duke out and locks the door behind him.)

JUVE: Sister Teresa, swear to me by the crucified God that what you say is true.

SISTER TERESA: I swear, Mr. Juve. The body that I watched over, concealed beneath this blanket, was that of a man.

JUVE: I believe you, Sister. There's a terrible mystery here.

SISTER TERESA: I believe so, too, Mr. Juve.

RUY: At your service—

JUVE: You also said that the body of the Duke was here—and that, without knowing how, it was transformed into that of a woman—into that of the Duchess—isn't that true?

RUY: Exactly.

JUVE: You didn't leave here for a minute?

SISTER TERESA(imprudently): Not me.

JUVE: Ah—what about you?

RUY: Only for a moment. I felt a need, and went to find Leopold to get something to drink.

SISTER TERESA: That's true. I wanted to pray alone. The central lights went out—leaving only the table lamp. A bit later, Mr. Juez arrived. You know the rest.

JUVE: We're getting there. (turning out the central lights leaving the table lamp) So you would have seen someone entering, right?

SISTER TERESA: Yes, certainly.

JUVE (by the light): You didn't fall asleep by chance?

SISTER TERESA: Well, I did feel a bit drowsy because of the heat, but I recovered immediately, and noticed this balcony was closed.

JUVE: It was closed? *Closed?* Did you open it?

SISTER TERESA: Yes, sir. I opened it; it was always open except in this moment when it was closed.

JUVE: Ah-ha! (going to the balcony, opens and closes it) What position was the other body in? Was it like this—shoulders toward the balcony.

BOTH: Yes, sir.

(A door can be seen opening discreetly.)

JUVE: Let's see.... Ah, Leopold. What about the Duke?

LEOPOLD: Gone to bed.

JUVE: Very good. Is there some other door besides the main door in the bedroom of your employer?

LEOPOLD: No, sir. Only there's a balcony on the other side of the park.

JUVE: Ruy, go and hold the door of the Lord Duke— with your revolver within easy reach.

RUY: It shall be done.

JUVE: You, Leopold, take a walk around the house and verify if this balcony is as described. If you see anything unusual, use this whistle.

(Juve gives Leopold a whistle.)

LEOPOLD: Right away.

(He leaves.)

JUVE: You, Sister Teresa, pray while I decipher this puzzle—let's see... The balcony was closed to anyone who wasn't aware you had opened it. Then this balcony is the thread leading to the drama. The solution to the mystery... (Goes to balcony and opens it.) Facing—a vacant hotel. (Pause. He turns his back to the balcony and looks at an almanac.) Hey, hey, Tuesday the Thirteenth. What a coincidence.

SISTER TERESA: The Thirteenth, you say. That's the number the Duchess had clutched in her hand.

JUVE: The same as Count d'Arley? No one told me!

SISTER TERESA: Mr. Juez forgot about it.

JUVE: These coincidences are very suggestive. Thirteen on the letter, thirteen in the almanac. Two crimes each linked to and near each other. This is getting complicated... Sister Teresa, do you know who's going to be that author of all this?

SISTER TERESA: Who?

JUVE: Fantômas.

SISTER TERESA: Hail Mary!

JUVE(goes to balcony and closes it) Eh—what's this? Let's see... Here's a projectile embedded... Here it is. I've got it. See, Sister Teresa—it's a steel bullet! This is the bullet that killed—who? The Duke's alive. The Duchess died by dagger. This bullet—this bullet—there's no doubt. It came from an air-gun of some sort—and was fired from this vacant house. It got embedded in the almanac after piercing the body of someone. But who? Yes, this is the clue! Pray, Sister, Teresa, pray. I am going to meditate, to squeeze my brain, to puzzle out this horrible plot, this awful machination, worthy only of a genius, a genius of evil—of Fantômas!

(Sits at the table, lights and smokes a cigar , and watches the puffs of smoke.)

SISTER TERESA(praying): Our father who art in Heaven—

CURTAIN

ACT II

The Gardens of Princess Lionelle. A beautiful illuminated park. A large pavilion. Multi-colored lights. A masked ball is in progress. There are several guests dressed as Fantômas, Harlequin and Pierrot. The effect is dazzling, kaleidoscopic and almost hallucinogenic.

GAMER: Beautiful Princess, your party is a dream. A story from The Arabian Nights.

LAMERIT: It's worthy of Marie Antoinette.

PRINCESS: Oh, for god's sake, dear friends. I only tried to hide, conceal, so to speak, the charitable intent, so as to get you to all come willingly, and without fear.

GAMER: I got it in every line. Your charity party has been attended by the most notable people in England

PRINCESS: Oh, yes, I am satisfied and grateful.

LAMERIT: And on the subject of unmasking—who is it who's masked like Fantômas that he passes so arrogantly through your park?

PRINCESS: It's your colleague, the Minister of Justice, Sir Edeval.

GAMER: Let's go there; on account of being incapable of catching this ghostly Fantômas—he dresses in his outfit.!

LAMERIT: Actually there are three of them—but the only true one exists. You have no opinion on the matter?

PRINCESS: None at all.

GAMER: As I was saying, it's been a long time that this monster, this atrocious criminal, exists only in the imagination of Inspector Juve, and the Minister of Justice.

EDEVAL: You are mistaken, dear colleague. (raising his hood) A thousand pardons, Princess.

PRINCESS: You're forgiven. But come closer and tell us some of his extraordinary adventures.

EDEVAL: With great pleasure. But I may indeed be able to present him to Your Highness this very evening.

PRINCESS: What are you saying? How? In my house? In the midst of my party?

EDEVAL: Yes, here, in the midst of this ball.

GAMER: Friend Edeval, you put our heart in a flutter. Ha, ha, ha, are you so gracious!

EDEVAL: With all due respect, I affirm that Fantômas exists and that, at some point, we will meet him among us.

LAMERIT: Near the Princess?

PRINCESS: We are going to see. (takes the card) Jesus! (after opening it) What does this mean? Look at this gentlemen?

GAMER: The Number 13 followed by a question mark, and below in very large letters, "Fantômas kisses the hand of Your Highness, and begs the help of the Minister of Justice to convince his colleague of the Interior that his existence is indisputable."

EDEVAL: What do you say to this? What do you say now?

GAMER: That it's a joke of great cleverness, well conceived, but carried out, in the end, by another of the masked men around here.

EDEVAL: That's fine. And is this the card that you received this morning. Look at the Number Thirteen, and after that listen (reading) "If the Lord Minister of Justice continues to want to see Fantômas, hurry tonight to the ball of Princess Lionelle. There we will see each other. Fantômas."

LAMERIT: Bah! It's from some lady who wants to meet you and has employed this means to attract you to this ball.

EDEVAL: You are incredible!

PRINCESS: Fine, friend Edeval—cover yourself with that hood and give me your arm—I want to calm my guests who have seen you in this costume and are frightened but intrigued, desiring to know who you are.

EDEVAL: With great pleasure. (covering up) But, wait a minute, Princess. I see there one of my agents. I'm going to give him some orders and change the search.

PRINCESS: Don't take too long.

(Edeval goes to talk to a Harlequin.)

PRINCESS: And the rest of you gentlemen, flit over to the salon, to wear out hearts.

LAMERIT: Your Highness is the one who subdues them at all hours.

(At this moment a Fantômas dressed exactly like Edeval emerges and gestures for the Princess to take his arm.)

PRINCESS: Thank God. I thought that Fantômas had robbed me of my gentle cavalier.

EDEVAL (finishes instructing his Harlequin) At your orders, Princess. Where'd she go? Bah! No doubt they've played an innocent joke on me. Since I'm here, I bet that the real Fantômas won't enter without my seeing him.

(He mixes in the crowd that goes into the park.)

MARQUISE (laughing): I told him that my beloved Marquis dances in an execrable way.

MARQUIS: My friend, the years don't go by for nothing, and little by little you lose the beat.

MARQUISE: That makes a bad dancer.

MARQUIS: But I'm still your best friend.

MARQUISE: I believe that, and you are going to give me a proof of it right now.

MARQUIS: Agreed!

MARQUISE: You see that gentleman dressed as Fantômas?

MARQUIS: Yes.

MARQUISE: He's the Minister of Justice.

MARQUIS: And what of it?

MARQUISE: Go to him and on some pretext catch him by the arm, bring him to the game room—he's a great chess player—invite him—

MARQUIS: He interests you so much?

MARQUISE: Very much!

MARQUIS: It shall be done. Till later, Marquise.

MARQUISE: Till later, Marquis.

(Pause)

(He takes the arm of the Minister of Justice who has gone into the pavilion.)

MARQUISE: No time to lose. (reads card) Black Pierrot with white pompoms. That's the one. He's coming to me. Thirteen?

PIERROT: Here and everywhere. (low) The Duchess?

MARQUISE: Traveling in India.

PIERROT: The business?

MARQUISE: Finished.

PIERROT: Fine. Don't lose sight of this window. And when the moment of tumult comes, watch below and spot him and throw him some Harlequin mask—here's the one you are waiting for. See!

(Another Harlequin enters.)

MARQUISE: He's not a Police Agent?

PIERROT: He is. But an agent in our power. Harlequin is Number Seven. Have you forgotten anything?

MARQUISE: Nothing at all.

PIERROT: Thirteen?

MARQUISE: Here and everywhere.

(Harlequin vanishes.)

I don't know what's going to happen. We will be ready

MARQUISE: for anything. Let's be alert. Eh?

(A second Harlequin enters. She lowers her fan.)

MARQUISE (aside): Who is he? (starting to go) No—
I'm staying here—at my post.

(The Fantômas that gave the Princess his arm approaches.)

FANTÔMAS: Thirteen.

MARQUISE: Here and everywhere.

(The Fantômas gives her the jewelry he has stolen from
the Princess. The Marquise puts it in her skirt. The
Fantômas throws a ball to the Second Harlequin who
catches it-then disappears.)

MARQUISE: Done. Now up and see what's going on.

(Gamer, Lamerit and other masks enter.)

GAMER: What daring! What audacity!

LAMERIT: It's uncanny.

MARQUISE: What happened, gentlemen?

GAMER: A stupendous thing.

LAMERIT: Unheard of!

MARQUISE: But what is it?

GAMER: Why, simply that Princess Lionelle was de-
spoiled of all her jewels in front of all the world.

LAMERIT: Right under our noses.

MARQUISE: But how was it done?

GAMER: The Princess was waltzing with the Minister
of Police. Suddenly, as if struck by a thunderbolt, she
fell fainting to the ground falling on her dancing partner.
We sought to help, as was natural, but as we pushed our
way into the tumult of masks of all classes prowling
around us, we became separated—and when we were

able to reach the side of the Princess, she'd been deposited on a sofa by the Minister, who had since disappeared along with her necklace and many jewels. Where is the Minister?

LAMERIT: And where are the jewels?

GAMER: They're bringing the Princess here. Come, Madame.

(Helped by various ladies the Princess is led in.)

LAMERIT: The heat in the ballroom is so excessive. We're bringing her here to see if she will recover.

(They find a seat for her.)

GAMER: Very well done! Give her air! Someone get a doctor!

MARQUISE (to Gamer): What disguise is the Minister of Justice wearing?

GAMER: He's here as Fantômas.

MARQUISE: Ah—then I saw him in the game room playing with my husband.

GAMER: Impossible!

MARQUISE: He's there, I tell you.

GAMER: Lamerit, go find him!

LAMERIT: Right away.

(he goes)

MARQUISE: That changes everything.

PRINCESS: My God! What happened to me? Who is this?

GAMER: Calm yourself, Princess. What happened? Nothing happened.

PRINCESS: What? My necklace, my bracelets, my earrings! Robbed! I've been robbed.

(Enter Edeval and Lamerit.)

GAMER: By whom, Madame, by whom?

PRINCESS(seeing Edeval): By this wretch! By this bandit!

EDEVAL: Me?

PRINCESS: Yes, you. (bitterly) My gentle cavalier.

EDEVAL: Madame, explain yourself, please.

GAMER: Princess, your accusation is very grave.

PRINCESS: Fine—Since then, no one has seen me separated from his arm. I was waltzing with him. He didn't leave me for a moment.

ALL: For sure!

EDEVAL(very firm): That's not so. You are mistaken. I call for the testimony of the Marquis de Grantley. Tell everyone here where you met me when you invited me to play cards!

MARQUIS: Here!

ALL: Here!

MARQUIS: Exactly!

EDEVAL: I told Your Highness that I was going to give some order, which I did, at the entrance of the Park. Having given them and returned, I found you had gone. Then, the Marquis invited me. I went with him to the game room where I stayed until just now. Refer to the testimony of those who were there. Isn't that true, gentlemen?

VARIOUS: It's true.

GAMER: Therefor, Princess, to which of us did you give your arm? With whom were you dancing?

PRINCESS: That's my question, my God!

LACKEY: For Her Highness—

(He presents a tray.)

PRINCESS: Let's see. A sort of ring and a card rolled up inside it! Yes, Number Thirteen? And beneath it. "Fantômas will not forget tonight's waltz."

EDEVAL: Who gave you this?

SERVANT: A mask dressed like your ladyship.

EDEVAL: From Fantômas?

PRINCESS: This is it?

EDEVAL: Lock all the gates of the Park. Five thousand pounds to whoever presents me a mask dressed as I am—dead or alive. That mask is Fantômas. Madame, , allow Mr. Lamerit to telephone to the palace of the Duke de Guerin, and order Commissioner Juez and Inspector Juve to come immediately.

PRINCESS: Give the orders you please.

EDEVAL (to Lamerit): You heard me. I guarantee you all that this Fantômas will fall into my power. Are you feeling better, Madame?

PRINCESS: Yes, I'm calming down. But Mr. Edeval—I owe you a thousand pounds for what I said previously.

EDEVAL: Princess, I won't accept this pardon until I can place the cause of all this at your feet.

LAMERIT: Inspector Juve is coming.

EDEVAL: Thank you. Until he gets here, gentlemen, I request everyone to take off their masks. In a case like this, I desire to know what people are prowling around.

(all obey)

EDEVAL: Thanks you everyone; I see that I am among friends.

HARLEQUIN: Inspector Juve is here.

EDEVAL: Let him come immediately. And don't let anyone leave on any pretext whatsoever.

HARLEQUIN: Understood.

JUVE (entering hat in hand): I was ordered to come. Here I am. What happened?

EDEVAL: What happened is this: Fantômas—disguised like me—introduced himself here and, boldly, by means almost supernatural, took my place near the Princess, with whom he danced while robbing her at the same time.

PRINCESS: Before leaving, he gave me this card.

JUVE (examines it): How much time has passed since this occurred?

EDEVAL: About an hour.

JUVE: Call the agent who opened the Park gate for me. Do you trust him?

EDEVAL: Completely.

JUVE (to Harlequin who enters): Has anyone left?

HARLEQUIN: No.

JUVE: Fine. You can go back to your station,

(The Harlequin leaves.)

JUVE: Have you made a search of the palace?

EDEVAL: Not yet. But I just offered 5000 pounds to whoever brings me dead or alive the aforesaid mask. And several went in search of him.

JUVE: But no one found anything, right?

EDEVAL: No one.

JUVE: The Princess has kept a list of her guests?

PRINCESS: It should be in the hand of the usher who announced them.

JUVE: I need that list. And pardon me, but it is necessary that I verify from it the identity of everyone here.

PRINCESS: Let Maurier come.

(Some go to find him.)

JUVE: A thousand thank yous, Madame.

(Maurier enters)

PRINCESS: Obey the gentleman in all he orders.

JUVE (to Maurier): According to Madame, you have the list of guests who were invited to this party?

MAURIER: Yes, sir. Here it is. The cross indicates the gentleman or lady was present. I always place this cross after announcing them.

JUVE: That's wonderful. So, those that do not have a cross—

MAURIER: They didn't come.

JUVE: That's it. Here we see Count d'Arley.

PRINCESS: The list was made before the occurrence of that unfortunate event.

JUVE: I understand. The Duke de Guerin. It's clear in this case it would be the same (reading further) Ah, he was here?

ALL: What?

JUVE: They didn't advise you that yesterday the Prince of York left for his estates in Germany?

PRINCESS, GAMER, OTHERS: That's true!

JUVE: Then who was the person Maurier crossed off?

MAURIER: I recall perfectly that I announced him.

JUVE: Bravo! You don't, by chance, recall his costume?

MAURIER (thinking): No, I don't remember.

JUVE: Fine—So we must inquire who in the house of the Princess gave or sold his or her invitation. Be calm, Princess. I will recover your jewels. I'm going to work on it.

GAMER: That's admirable.

EDEVAL (to Juve): I take a great interest, friend Juve, in your victory.

JUVE: It will come when it comes, Minister.

(Commotion off.)

EDEVAL: What's going on?

GAMER: What uproar is this?

1st GENTLEMAN: Minister, they've caught him.

2nd GENTLEMAN: He's in our power.

EDEVAL: Who? Fantômas? Alive?

1st GENTLEMAN: We found him dead, at the foot of the wall in the park. They're bringing him here.

EDEVAL: In the end, he's ours.

(They bring in a body dressed as Fantômas.)

EDEVAL: Get back, everybody! I want to be the first to pull this cursed hood from his face.

(He removes the hood.)

EDEVAL: The Duke de Guerin!

JUVE: Who? (looking) My God! It's him! The Duke! But, Minister, this man cannot be the Duke. The Duke is in his palace. I just left him there.

EDEVAL(to Lamerit): Telephone the Duke de Guerin.

LAMERIT: Right away.

JUVE (hand on the head of the cadaver): Hear me, Minister. Hear me, everyone. I swear to you on the head of this cadaver, on the salvation of my soul—that Fantômas is not dead.

CURTAIN

ACT III

The same set as Act I. The same night as Act II. The Duke is on the telephone. Nothing has changed. Only the body of the Duchess has been removed.

DUKE: Yes, I am. And you are Juve? Fine. Greet him in my name? What's happened? Right, it's too big a thing to discuss on the telephone. Fine, I can wait without going to bed until you return. Yes, Goodbye, thanks.
(He rings a bell.)
LEOPOLD: Did you call, Milord?
DUKE: Yes, Leopold. When Mr. Juve comes in, let me know. Meanwhile, don't let anyone bother me.
LEOPOLD: As you order.
DUKE: You may withdraw.
(Leopold bows and leaves. The Duke locks the door after him, and turns off the central light. Only the red light on the table is on. He goes straight to the library next to the chimney and removes a large book. He presses a spring in the space from which the book was removed and the secret door opens. A Pierrot and a Masked Fantômas appear.)
DUKE: Ah, there you are. Is it you?
PIERROT: Yes, Chief.
DUKE: What happened?
PIERROT: Everything worked as we planned and expected.
FANTÔMAS: I took the place of that stupid Minister of Police.
DUKE: What about the jewels?
PIERROT: Here they are.
DUKE: Let's have a look.

(He examines them with expertise and satisfaction. Pause.)

DUKE: Indeed, these are the jewels of a real princess. The trick worked. This necklace, this bracelet and these earrings, are worth more than 700,000 pounds.

PIERROT, FANTÔMAS: Magnificent.

DUKE: Have this taken to the treasury of our association. We are very rich.

PIERROT: Thanks, Chief, to your unquestionable talent.

FANTÔMAS: To your valor, to your audacity.

DUKE: Bah! It's nothing. Changing the subject—the Duchess?

PIERROT: All orders complied with, as always. She's traveling in India.

DUKE: From where she won't return, certainly.

PIERROT: I'm not very easy about that, Chief. I think we ought to kill her.

DUKE: That's not necessary. Besides, you know she cared for and closed the eyes of my poor mother. You must learn to know how to be grateful. She has returned the favor. I won't put out hers.

FANTÔMAS: The second part of our work tonight was accomplished without a misstep. From our companions Number 1 and 3 we received this and I got over the wall of the Princess's Park. We left the corpse of the Duke of Guerin dressed in one of our outfits, with your card in his pocket. As to the rest—

DUKE: I understand. The Minister of Police read my card and, like everyone else, thinks that Fantômas is dead.

FANTÔMAS: Almost everyone. Juve didn't believe it.

DUKE: Ah, that's because Juve has great talent. You know him. He's a worthy adversary, who's done his best

to get rid of me. The look alike Fantômas with the Duke produced—
PIERROT: A tremendous effect.
DUKE: On Juve?
PIERROT: Juve didn't emerge from his amazement.
DUKE: Bravo! Very soon he'll be given the solution to all of it. Tell the Marquise to come see me immediately—but not here—(points to chimney) By the main door, like a visitor with all respect. Take these jewels. Give them to the Treasurer, and advise all the companions so that in the morning there'll be no mistakes. The robbery of this Princess can end our association. We are immensely rich. Tomorrow, distribute 50 million francs between the twelve companions. I, with the fortune of the Duke de Guerin ,that belongs to me by law, and the 20 million remaining—I believe I can live a perfectly satisfactory life.
PIERROT & FANTÔMAS: Long live Fantômas!
DUKE: Christ! Silence, my friends! Don't you know that, as of today, Fantômas is dead.
(They leave by the way they came. The Duke paces up and down pondering the situation.)
DUKE: There's no other remedy. I've got to kill Juve. Let's decide how...
LEOPOLD (entering): Milord?
DUKE: What is it?
LEOPOLD: Mr. Juve is here.
DUKE: Bring him in immediately.
(Juve enters.)
DUKE: Oh, friend Juve, I'm dying of anticipation— what happened?
JUVE (calmly): A small thing. The Princess Lionelle was robbed of a necklace, earrings, and a bracelet worth 800,000 pounds.

DUKE: Almost a million.

JUVE: Almost a million, yes. As you can see, the strike was a good one, but I will quickly recover the jewels.

DUKE: Are you sure of that?

JUVE: I have the evidence.

DUKE: Be tireless!

JUVE: I will do my duty. But the most extraordinary thing about tonight—isn't this—

DUKE: There's more?

JUVE: And so natural a thing that unless the Minister of Police is deceived, Fantômas is dead.

DUKE (very surprised): What? Are you certain?

JUVE: So it seems. But what's happening Milord, are you ill?

DUKE: No, it's nothing—a passing faintness. And you say that—what proofs do you have of his death?

JUVE: The best of all—his own body.

DUKE(feverish): Are you certain?

JUVE: I myself saw him.

DUKE: And this man?

JUVE: This man seems to be an extraordinary man?

DUKE (sobbing): He is—My God!

(falling in the arm chair)

JUVE: Say, Milord, could you explain to me...?

DUKE: Yes, friend Juve. Yes—doubt is impossible, another new blow has sorrowed my heart.

JUVE: How?

DUKE: The man you've seen is Fantômas—I'm sure of it.

JUVE: And how do you know that?

DUKE: Because, Juve, to get to the point, though I blush to confess it, this man, this wretch, this thief, this assassin, this abortion from Hell—this Fantômas—is my brother.

JUVE (astonished): Your brother!

DUKE: To my great shame.

JUVE: I can't get over my amazement.

DUKE: We were both born in the Castle of Guerin, the same day; we are twins. Our father was absent for months because of the war with Russia. For a year we didn't hear any good news. The war prevented all kinds of communications. Nomad tribes were continually crossing the country in search of better living conditions, and one of them stole my brother. One day, I returned to Castle Guerin in the desolate arms of the nurse maid—we weren't even two years-old. Six months later, they made peace, and my father announced his arrival; my dear mother, to prevent her beloved husband from experiencing tremendous disappointment, presented him with only one son—me. She hid the existence of the other from him.

JUVE: But...

DUKE: The servants were dismissed and paid in gold.

JUVE: And after that—what?

DUKE: After that, years later, the leader of that tribe arrived to offer me the secret of my brother's life. I accepted with jubilation and had a meeting with him. My brother was a cynic, a criminal, a wretch. Only, he wanted money to keep his silence. Our father was dead. After that, petitions for money became more violent, his threats more terrible. Finally, getting tired of it—in love with the wife of his brother—he penetrated here, and, unable to achieve his infamous desires, stabbed her heart, as you saw, with his dagger.

(crying)

JUVE: But the proof of all this?

DUKE: It's here, in my desk.

JUVE: In your desk? I inspected your desk and saw nothing.

DUKE: They are locked in a secret drawer.

JUVE: Ah!

DUKE (pulling from the secret drawer a package of letters): Take a look. Here they are. Take them; you can examine them.

JUVE: Milord, I cannot cease to be astonished, and as you explain it—to what do you attribute his death?

DUKE: But I don't have the least doubt. His head had a price on it in many places. Some new Judas has collected his reward.

JUVE: It may be better than that, Milord, I imagine. It won't inconvenience you to make a written declaration about what you've just me? Which will remain with you along with this packet of letters.

DUKE: Count on it.

LEOPOLD (in the doorway): Excuse me, Milord.

DUKE: What is it?

LEOPOLD: The Marquise de Grantley insists on seeing his Lordship.

JUVE: The Marquise—at this hour!

DUKE: It's almost twelve at night. Show her in. Nothing unusual for you at all; she was at the ball, right?

JUVE: Exactly.

DUKE: You can stay. The Marquise's been close for many years. Very tender bonds united us. Can you understand?

JUVE: Understood.

MARQUISE (entering): My beloved Duke.

DUKE: My dear friend! I am informed about it.

MARQUISE: Informed—by whom?

DUKE: By my friend, Mr. Juve.

MARQUISE: Ah, I didn't notice him—please excuse me. Mr. Juve.

DUKE: You can say anything before him! I just finished confessing everything to him.

MARQUISE: You will see that in the end that he deserved it.

DUKE: Yes, but he was my brother.

JUVE: With your permission, Milord, I'll take my leave now.

DUKE: I hoped to talk more—but come back soon.

JUVE: Shortly. Madame la Marquise.

(Juve inclines his head to the Marquise, then leaves. The Duke and the Marquise carefully inspect the room to make sure they are alone. Pause.)

DUKE: That man suspects. He must be killed.

MARQUISE: Order and you will be obeyed.

DUKE: Within an hour he will sit down at this desk to complete his report.

MARQUISE: And?

DUKE: You know how you killed the Duke?

MARQUISE: Yes.

DUKE: You will kill Juve in the same way.

MARQUISE: When?

DUKE: Within an hour.

(The Duke opens the door, and calls.)

DUKE: Leopold, accompany the Marquise!

(Leopold bows.)

MARQUISE: Goodbye, poor Duke! I sense your resignation.

(Juve reappears and watches.)

DUKE (having bid goodbye to the Marquise): The triumph is— (seeing Juve) Ah! What a fright you gave me, my dear Juve.

JUVE: What were you saying before about a triumph?

DUKE: Oh, that justice always triumphs.

JUVE: Without a doubt.

(Pause)

DUKE: Are you going to work tonight?

JUVE: Yes, it will take me, certainly, more than two hours.

DUKE: In that case, I'm leaving you, my friend. Till morning.

(rings bell)

JUVE: Sleep well.

DUKE: Thank you.

(The Duke and Leopold leave.)

JUVE: Can I doubt it? Is it true what this man said? Can I be accusing an innocent? No, my conscience is at peace. The trail is good. Let's compile my report and trust in Divine Providence. (sits at the table) I don't have the least doubt; his evidence fails to convince me. Oh, how entangled is the evidence...

(Enter Leopold)

JUVE: Is it you, Leopold? Be so good as to lock this door with the key that is there.

(Leopold takes the key and locks the door.)

JUVE: Very good. Tell Ruy to come.

LEOPOLD: With pleasure.

(Leopold leaves.)

JUVE: My game begins. I have the reputation of being a good gambler. We'll see about that.

RUY (in the doorway): May I?

JUVE: Please come in! Did you carry out my errand?

RUY: Scrupulously. I've spent all my time at the house opposite.

JUVE: And?

RUY: In the dust—on the patio, and on the landing of the stairway, and the upper living area—are the delicate footprints of a woman—admirably shod.

JUVE: Are you completely certain?

RUY: I'm sure. In the first part, the form of a delicate and fine footprint, the heel of a boot or shoe, Louis XV style, here's a sketch for you.

(giving him a sketch)

JUVE: All right.

RUY: The footprints end at the foot of the window which faces the balcony. Moreover...

JUVE: What?

On the window sill is a mark that is clearly the mark of a stick, a wide stick, as if it was the place where a stick was put.

JUVE: Or a rifle with a scope!

RUY: Yes, sir.

JUVE: Bravo, Ruy! Success is going to crown our efforts. Not a word of this to anyone—to anyone. Before you go, open this window, the heat is unendurable.

(Ruy goes to the balcony and starts opening the windows.)

RUY: Mr. Juve...

JUVE: What is it?

RUY: I've just seen something extraordinary.

JUVE: Speak quickly.

RUY: I've just seen, in the house facing this one, in the room facing this one—a woman entered with a candle and put it out quickly.

JUVE: Get down (kneeling) Listen.

RUY (kneeling also): I'm all ears.

(They withdraw from the balcony.)

JUVE: Go see Leopold and get a silk kerchief.

(Ruy leaves.)

JUVE: The events are coming together. I am probably in danger of death. No room for doubt now. They want to kill me—like the other one. But we will see, my friends, we will see!

(Ruy returns.)

RUY: Here it is.

JUVE: You know what a scarecrow is, right? Then knot this kerchief around this plaster bust of Nelson sitting on the mantelpiece. Meanwhile I'll put out the light and move the chair. Let's get to work.

(He puts out the main lights, creeps to the balcony and opens the window without raising more than his arm.)

JUVE: Now.

(Ruy follows his instructions.)

JUVE: Perfect. Let's place it on the desk—with all sorts of precautions. There. Let me move the chair a little. See—it looks like a person who's fallen asleep at the desk, writing; me, for example. (pause) Now, take three men and, without causing any disturbance, go and arrest the bird who is in the house opposite. Dead or alive. And bring her to me immediately.

(Ruy leaves.)

JUVE: Now to turn the lights back on. Let's see what happens.

(Pause. He turns the light back on. He smokes without losing sight of the bust from a position that cannot be seen from the balcony. Suddenly, there is a crack. The bust shatters.)

JUVE: Great shot. If I'd been there, I'd be a dead man.

(He picks up the head and examines it.)

JUVE: Yes, here's the bullet. Exactly the same as the first. Now let's wait. (pause) They're here. They've arrived. Come in!

(Ruy enters with three men holding a woman prisoner; she wears a hood hiding her identity.)

RUY: The bird's been caught.

JUVE: See if she's armed!

RUY: She doesn't have more weapons than this plaything. It's a compressed air gun.

(He takes it from one of the police men holding it.)

JUVE (examining it): Magnificent example. A true precision weapon. (to the Marquise) Madame, I congratulate you. (to the policemen) You can withdraw but always stay within call. (to the Marquise again) Sit down, Madame, and take off your hood. It will make you sweat.

(The Marquise sits and angrily removes her hood.)

JUVE: Damn! The Marquise de Grantley!

MARQUISE: The same, sir, the same!

JUVE: Madame, how much were you offered to kill me? Because I imagine you don't intend to deny it.

MARQUISE: Absolutely not. I feel like a guilty woman in a mousetrap. The jealous are guilty.

JUVE: The jealous! You were jealous of me?

MARQUISE: I was—of the Duke.

JUVE: Ah, it was the Duke you killed—By what chance have you dedicated yourself to killing Dukes?

MARQUISE: I don't understand.

JUVE: Enough farces! The one you intended to kill was me. Don't deny it, I'm convinced of it.

MARQUISE: You are mistaken, Mr. Juve. You've done nothing to me. Whereas, the Duke—

JUVE: No doubt you didn't want to lose him, and because of jealousy, the cursed jealousy—that's not badly contrived. We shall see if the judges appreciate your talent for fiction.

MARQUISE: The judges. Why should I be judged?

JUVE: Be certain you will be—if we cannot reach an understanding.

MARQUISE: An understanding about what? In what way?

JUVE: I've got indubitable proof that this is the second time you shot this neat toy, from the opposite house, at your chosen victim. The first time you fired, you hit a man; this time, the man was a plaster head. These two feats weren't done for your own pleasure, they were accomplished by order of a supreme leader—Fantômas!

MARQUISE: False, I don't know him.

JUVE: You belong to Fantômas' gang. Whose aforesaid gang, disguised as ambulatory artisans, works from towns to cities. In it, you were amazing because of your skill at marksmanship. You announced yourself like an American woman and your marvelous shots were applauded. Much later, you stumbled onto the old Marquis de Grantley, and soon you became his legitimate wife. So you see, Madame la Marquise, the police are not all as naive as they seem.

MARQUISE: And what does seeing all this result in?

JUVE: A lot. You've been, perhaps, one of the principal members of the gang. I promise you freedom and silence—in exchange for you being expansive in your declarations.

MARQUISE: Never!

JUVE: Think very carefully—

MARQUISE: Anything before treason.

JUVE: Ah! So, it's certain you will ruin yourself?

MARQUISE: For whom? For Fantômas? With him, body and soul. You know it. Let me go.

JUVE: Are you crazy? You'll leave here, but you're going to prison.

MARQUISE: Who, me? The Marquise of Grantley. But, you—you want to make yourself ridiculous?

JUVE: The Marquise of Grantley has been caught in flagrante delicto of attempted murder—and consequently—

(going to her)

MARQUISE: Be still—don't forget I am a woman capable of murder.

(grabs the lamp on the table)

JUVE (revolver in hand): Careful what you do, Madame. It would displease me greatly to be obliged to shoot your delicate body.

MARQUISE: Before that, I'll save myself. Save me, Fantômas.

(She puts out the lights. The chimney opens and Fantômas pulls her away.)

JUVE: Treachery! Ruy! Everyone come here! Lights! Lights!

(He fumbles around trying to find the light switch, and after getting the lights working, opens the door.)

JUVE: Gone! Gone! But where?

(Ruy enters with an officer.)

JUVE: This door—locked—the other that I opened. Maybe the balcony. (going to balcony) Impossible. She would have been killed. Run. Search everywhere.

(The police leave.)

JUVE: It must be admitted that Fantômas is the genius of evil—what a genius! The only proof that I had in my power, he just snatched from me. I confess my error. They wanted to assassinate me by the same means as the Duke. By the same path, the Marquise disappeared, so this means they took the first cadaver and arranged it like the other. The story of the brother is surely a great fabrication. And the one who lives must be the bandit who supplanted his brother. Yes, there's no doubt—I see it plainly now. But the proof—the proof... Where is the evidence that supports all this reasoning. Where is it? Where to find it?

(The telephone rings)

JUVE: Yes. Juve speaking. What? A telegram? For me? Who is it from? Did you open it? No? I still haven't gotten it.

(Ruy enters with telegram.)

JUVE: Ah, yes, they've brought it just now. Thanks! Bye!

(to Ruy)

JUVE: Bring it here! What can it be?

(opening and reading it)

JUVE: What does it say? Yes! Yes, this is it! The proof! Here is the proof! Ruy, don't leave here until I return. I've got him in my power. The proof so much desired. Look, read, and don't forget.

RUY (reading): Oh, Mr. Juve, this is marvelous.

JUVE (taking another look at the telegram): Marvelous, yes—so unexpected—the proof. Like it is here. The proof, undisputable, palpable. You're mine, Fantômas, you're mine!

CURTAIN

ACT IV

Same as preceding act. Day.

DUKE (writing): My good Leopold, in this document I name you my general administrator during the time of my voyage to Russia. I'll leave this morning—You will secure and guard this palace until my return I will provide you with some necessary money to cover all expenses—And on my return I'll know how to reward your good services.

LEOPOLD: Milord!

DUKE: Every day take a wreath of fresh flowers to the tomb of the Duchess.

LEOPOLD: I will, Milord.

DUKE: And now, let's shake hands, I'm going to leave immediately. Mr. Juve hasn't returned?

LEOPOLD: No, Milord.

DUKE: Fine. Let's shake again.

(Leopold leaves)

DUKE: What happened? That Juve isn't here seems shocking to me. Bah! tonight all that remains is to dissolve the association—and Fantômas will have quite simply disappeared.

(Leopold returns.)

LEOPOLD; Someone's brought this card, Milord.

(holds out a tray)

DUKE: Do they want a reply? Who brought it?

LEOPOLD: A delivery man I don't know.

DUKE: You may withdraw.

(Leopold leaves.)

DUKE: The letter appears to be from the Marquise. We are going to see what happened. "Dear Duke, come to see me. Distrust all."

(He reads it pensively. Then he burns the letter calmly and rings the bell. Leopold returns.)

DUKE: The car?

LEOPOLD: It's ready, Milord.

DUKE: Let's go.

(He leaves with Leopold. After a moment, Ruy enters from the opposite direction, with Juve and the Duchess.)

RUY: This way is clear.

JUVE: Discard all fear, Madame. We are alone.

DUCHESS: Thank you, my friend.

JUVE: I am fulfilling my duty. I understand all the sorrow that you'll have at the sight of this place after all that's occurred, but it is necessary in order to complete the punishment of the guilty.

DUCHESS: I am ready for anything.

JUVE: The information you gave me clarifies all the truth. What I don't understand is the infamous mutilation of your right hand.

DUCHESS: It's very simple—this ring was placed in my right hand with the escutcheon of my ancestors. It was necessary to join this hand to the wax mannequin, to call attention to it, to place the paper with the Number Thirteen, and to avoid the discovery of the wax figure by reclaiming it, thus avoiding an autopsy which would reveal it was a mannequin.

JUVE: It's true. All is perfectly explained.

DUCHESS: My friend, I am faint. In the long and hurried journey with these infamous ones, my flight through the fields put me under the protection of the authorities, and now, this no less precipitous return has exhausted all my energy.

JUVE: Ruy, fly below and bring something up; Madame Duchess needs food.

RUY: I'm going and I'll be back in a flash.

(Pause)

JUVE: According to what you told me before—there's a secret entry in this office through which we can go back—can you show me the place where—?

(The Duchess faints.)

JUVE: Eh! What's this? (speaking to her respectfully) Madame la Duchesse! Madame la Duchesse! (aside) She's fainted. (going to the door) Ruy! Ruy! (aside) He doesn't hear me. That's obvious. He's downstairs in the kitchen. What did I see. Ah, yes—in the bedroom. Water at the head of the bed. Let's run.

(He goes out. Immediately the secret chimney door opens and two masked Fantômas and the Marquise, veiled, dressed exactly like the Duchess emerge. The Fantômases take the Duchess and disappear. The Marquise assumes the position and attitude of the Duchess as Juve returns.)

JUVE: Here it is. Found this flask of salts, too—on the table. I'm going to see if it revives her breathing.

MARQUISE (gun in hand): Mr. Juve, not a word, not a gesture.

JUVE: What? (stupefied) Am I dreaming?

MARQUISE: Give me the revolver you carry—immediately.

JUVE: But—

(reacting)

MARQUISE: Be careful. Don't forget I hold your life in my hands.

JUVE: Here's my revolver.

MARQUISE: A thousand thanks. Now go sit in that chair.

(He does.)

MARQUISE: So, now Mr. Juve, we are going to chat.

JUVE (sarcastic):I consider myself very honored. But what if Ruy comes?

MARQUISE: Ruy will get exactly the same as you.

JUVE: Fine, then let's get this over with quickly.

MARQUISE: I imagine that you recognize me?

JUVE (sarcastic): I am one of the most fervent admirers of the celebrated Marquise de Grantley.

MARQUISE: I congratulate you on your memory. This veil was suffocating me. (removing the veil) My friend Juve, now we are face to face again.

JUVE: For me, it's an immense pleasure, but I supplicate you.

MARQUISE: I am not thinking of making you suffer much.

JUVE: What a kind heart you have!

MARQUISE: No. I have orders to offer you peace.

JUVE: Peace?

MARQUISE

Yes, with certain conditions and guarantees.

JUVE: You are giving conditions—to me?

MARQUISE: I can, I think. You are in my power. With a simple move of this finger, I can send you to eternity. Swear to me, on your honor that you'll leave the country in forty-eight hours, and tell me in what part of the world I can send you a check for a million pounds. I keep this revolver, and I will exchange it now for another check of fifty thousand pounds for your travel expenses. I won't come back ever to trouble police business. How's that seem?

JUVE: These are beautiful proposals.

MARQUISE: Truly?

JUVE: You have really dazzled me, and I do not dazzle easily—but I do not accept.

MARQUISE: Why don't you accept?

JUVE: What do you expect, Madame, it's a caprice of mine.

MARQUISE: But are you crazy? Don't you know that if you do not accept, I have orders to—?

JUVE: To kill me. That I know. I expected it.

MARQUISE: Then—

JUVE: Ah, Marquise, it would be a great pleasure for me to die by your sweet hands.

MARQUISE: You are very odd.

JUVE: It's the least that is permitted to one who is sentenced to death—oddness.

MARQUISE: Fine. Let's stick to the point. Yes or no?

JUVE: No.

MARQUISE: Have you thought carefully about it?

JUVE: Very carefully. Do your best without fear. It takes only a second, and with your recognized facility I hope to receive a bullet between the eyes.

MARQUISE: Then until eternity, friend Juve.

(The Duke appears, unseen by Juve, and with a gesture orders her not to shoot.)

JUVE: Until eternity, Marquise—why didn't you shoot?

MARQUISE: He ordered me not to.

JUVE: Mercy. What an opportunity. To arrive at such a critical moment.

DUKE (to Marquise): Did you write me a letter?

MARQUISE: I didn't write you anything.

JUVE: I wrote you—which is the same in this case. I needed to get Your Excellency away from here for a while.

DUKE: You could have saved yourself the trouble. I was about to leave.

JUVE: Could I have guessed it? We are almost at home. Watch this revolver, beloved Marquise, while we chat.

DUKE: What is—?

JUVE: My beloved Mr. Fantômas, keep calm. Yesterday, I listened to your excellent, detailed and partially true story of your family. I know, I repeat myself. You've made yourself in fact and in law, the Duke of Guerin. I know all your diabolical machinations to become Duke. I recognize your prodigious and criminal talent, and I want to be generous. I want to spare the noble family of de Guerin the infamy and horrible spectacle of seeing the last Duke executed in the public square. I've made a written report of your robberies and crimes, of the evil business you made with the name of Fantômas, and in which de Guerin does not figure at all. I am trusting you to take this revolver, which is on the seat of the chair, and blow off the top of your cranium. Are we in agreement?

DUKE: Are you crazy, Mr. Juve?

MARQUISE: What a good preacher you would make.

JUVE: Thank you for your kindness.

DUKE: Mr. Juve, you forget that you are dealing with Fantômas, and to know Fantômas is a sentence of death. By force of custom and constancy, you've learned it four times. Bah! What proof have you? If you were stupid enough to accuse me, you'd be laughed at. The Duke de Guerin is untouchable, and has nothing to do with your chimerical suspicions. You imagined for a moment that you held some proof in your power when you received a telegram that announced the Duchess was still alive— The Duchess, yes, that's what it was—but we snatched it from you—and the mannequin we used has disappeared, and her body will soon take its proper place, pierced in the heart by a mortal dagger thrust.

JUVE: What horror!

DUKE: So, you see, to mess with me, with Fantômas, is to go straight to death. You are in my power. I want to be generous like you and offer you life and a million pounds.

JUVE: It's certain now. I recognize that I am vanquished.

DUKE: Do you accept?

JUVE: What else can I do?

MARQUISE: At last!

JUVE: On one condition.

DUKE: Let's hear it.

JUVE: I want the whole amount in a single check. After I leave, I don't want to bother with this matter anymore.

DUKE: Agreed.

(The Duke goes to the desk and takes out a checkbook. To the Marquise)

DUKE: Give me the other.

MARQUISE: Here's yours.

DUKE: Where do you want to cash it?

JUVE: In Moscow. At the Bank of London.

DUKE: Perfect. Take it.

JUVE: Thank you, Milord. In the end, you've given me a powerful proof.

DUKE: What?

JUVE: Very simple. It will be necessary to compare your letter with that in the pocket of your poor brother. That, I can do.

MARQUISE: Ah, bandit!

(She goes to grab her revolver, but Juve more rapidly pulls one he has hidden.)

JUVE: Quiet, my beauty. The papers have been exchanged.

(The Duke goes for the gun on the desk.)

JUVE: Don't bother, Milord. It's an inoffensive weapon.

DUKE (examining it): Unloaded!

JUVE: What do you want, she took mine. All the words said here were heard by Mr. Juez, hidden behind this door. He's awaiting my invitation to take you. They accuse you also!

DUKE: Of what?

JUVE: I now know the secret passage that links that deserted house with this one, and which exits in your bedroom—that's how we got in. I know all the horrible plot surrounding the assassination of Count d'Arley. I know the clever plan for robbing the Princess Lionelle, and for the murder of your brother, in order to take his place, the abduction of the Duchess, and the celebrated wax mannequin—of all that a man is capable of—Fantômas—that is to say, you. But today you are the legitimate Duke of Guerin, and considering the nobility of this name, I offer to you for the last time my own revolver—so that you can blow your brains out.

DUKE: Never!

MARQUISE: Save yourself!

(She grabs Juve and won't let go.)

JUVE: Get back, Madame, let me go or I won't answer—

MARQUISE: Flee, Fantômas, Flee!

DUKE: You are mistaken, Marquise. I won't. What for? If they beat the doors down to enter—they won't find anything. Not even the body of Juve.

(The Duke presses the spring and the chimney door opens—two Masked Fantômases appear, revolvers in hand.)

DUKE: Mr. Juve has seized the hour of great decision (to the Fantômases.) One to the right, the other to the left of the gentleman. At the first movement, shoot him. (to

Juve) Mr. Juve, let's settle our accounts. I offered you what I could have avoided by murdering you, but you are a madman, enamored of death. There, you see, you are irrevocably lost. No matter—twice you offered me death. I don't want to do less and offer you life again.

JUVE: A thousand thanks, Milord. So much generosity confounds me, but—

DUKE: But what?

JUVE: But I'll leave peacefully to my home—meanwhile the Lord Duke—

DUKE: What—?

JUVE: —Will leave to the prison or to the cemetery.

DUKE (scornfully): Do you believe in miracles?

JUVE: Yes, Milord—not you?

DUKE: In other situations, but not this one.

JUVE: Now a miracle is going to be realized.

(stands up and orders the two Fantômases.)

JUVE: One to the right, the other to the left of this gentleman. At the first movement—shoot him.

(The two place themselves as directed and take off their masks.)

DUKE: Leopold!

MARQUISE: Ruy!

(The Duke flees to the chimney, opens the door, and locks it after him.)

JUVE: Seize this woman!

(They grab and disarm her. Juve opens the door and calls.)

JUVE: Grab them all, Mr. Juez—this way, this way, everyone. He's getting away!

(Juez and other policemen enter.)

JUVE: Run! Watch the exits of the uninhabited housed. I am going to enter it from the bedroom—this man is capable of anything. Try to save the Duchess.

(He listens by the chimney.)

JUVE: Quiet!

(All obey. The chimney door opens rapidly, and the Duke emerges, fleeing from the Duchess, who pursues him arrogantly, a revolver in her left hand and her right hand bandaged; behind the Duchess comes a police officer also with a gun in his hand.)

DUKE: It's she! She! The Duchess! She betrayed me.

JUVE: No, Milord. My agents invaded this place, secretly—before. They freed her and seized your accomplices. The swoon was feigned. You fell into a trap.

DUKE: Curses!

DUCHESS (very energetic and dignified): Die, Milord! If you are not a coward, save yourself from infamy—and the name of a noble family.

DUKE (taking the revolver the Duchess offers him): Ah, yes. Get back, swine. You cannot catch Fantômas unless he's dead.

(He shoots himself and falls at the feet of the Duchess.)

JUVE: You see, Fantômas, Justice always triumphs. Society can sleep peacefully; the genius of evil is dead. Mr. Juez, I give you—Fantômas!

CURTAIN

THE RESURRECTION OF FANTÔMAS

Part II of THE TRUMPH OF FANTÔMAS
by Jose Maria Martin de Eugenio
(1916)

CHARACTERS

The Marquise de Grantley
Margot
Princess Crostandy
Emilia
Mr. Regarden (Warden)
First Prison Guard
Second Prison Guard
Fantômas
Leonard Emmanuel
Mr. Juez (Police Commissioner)
Ruy (a police officer)
Inspector Juve
The Duke de Mirandela
Prince Crostandy
Gamer (a Minister)
False Gamer
Sir Edeval (Minister of Justice)
Doctor Gramendi
The Notary (M. de Samay)
Usher
Masked Fantômas, Gentlemen, Policemen

Act I and II take place in London in 1912; the rest around 1915.

ACT I

The Boudoir of an elegant young lady. The room has a balcony overlooking a large square. There is an armoire against one wall. A table is set lavishly with a dinner for two. It is night.

Regarden, the head of prison guards at London's prison, is talking with the Marquise de Grantley, who is wearing a shawl and a mask.

REGARDEN: We are agreed. We will risk our skin, but the reward is great.
MARQUISE: Five hundred thousand pounds.
REGARDEN: There's nothing more to say. The prisoner Fantômas will be in your arms between one and three this evening. And at four—
MARQUISE: I know—he will be executed.
REGARDEN: There's no other remedy.
(sound of hammers in the street)
REGARDEN: Those hammers indicate that the scaffold is being prepared.
MARQUISE: Go, and carry out the agreement. It's after midnight.
REGARDEN: I'm going to prepare the work. Meanwhile, my companions are here, watching the staircase and the balconies of the house. We didn't get anything from the lady—notwithstanding, we know her—her money is good—but Fantômas is capable of anything, even the most dangerous. What gave him the idea?
MARQUISE: Where'd he get it? Haven't you ever seen some criminal escape before his execution?
REGARDEN: Never in England.

MARQUISE: Now is the time.

REGARDEN: It doesn't matter. To change from your money, we are going to leave with you your relative or your lover the last two hours of his life. So we'll deserve the 500,000, but during these two hours we won't lose sight of the house, nor of him.

MARQUISE: You are perfectly within your right.

REGARDEN (saluting): At your service.

MARQUISE: Go with God!

(After Regarden leaves, the Marquise goes to the armoire and opens it.)

MARQUISE: Thirteen?

(A Masked Fantômas emerges from the armoire.)

MASKED FANTÔMAS: Here and everywhere.

(He unmasks.)

MARQUISE: What's to be done?

MASKED FANTÔMAS: Everything's going perfectly. The middle of the two houses are bored through. Communication expedited, the car is in the corner. The companions on the alert.

MARQUISE: Bravo! What about Number four?

MASKED FANTÔMAS: He's at his station, dressed in the livery of a rich house.

MARQUISE: Mighty fine. And the letter?

MASKED FANTÔMAS: Delivered.

MARQUISE: The narcotic?

MASKED FANTÔMAS: In the Spanish wine—a bottle of Sherry.

MARQUISE: Perfect.

MASKED FANTÔMAS: Any more orders, Madame la Marquise?

MARQUISE: No.

MASKED FANTÔMAS (saluting): Thirteen.

MARQUISE: Here and everywhere.

(The Masked Fantômas leaves.)

MARQUISE: The moment is coming. Nothing to worry about, we will triumph. Long live Fantômas! Hey!

(goes to balcony)

MARQUISE: They're coming out. They are taking him. That was foreseen. They didn't remove the handcuffs. What imbeciles! They'll regret this. But let's not anticipate.

(going to door, opening it, and listening)

MARQUISE: They're coming up. They're here.

REGARDEN: We are here, Madam.

(Two guards, Fantômas and Regarden enter.)

MARQUISE: I imagine that you don't object to my asking them to remove the handcuffs?

REGARDEN: Not at all, Madam.

(The guards do it.)

MARQUISE (handing the money): Count it; I've added a thousand more to the agreed sum. Take it.

(He takes it.)

MARQUISE: Well—it's correct?

REGARDEN: Everything is in order. (to the guards) Let's go. At three exactly, we will rap on this door.

MARQUISE: And I will open to you at three exactly.

(She closes the door behind them. Fantômas looks around. She removes her mask.)

FANTÔMAS: You!

MARQUISE: Yes, me. My beloved Fantômas!

(She embraces him.)

FANTÔMAS: Will you explain?

MARQUISE: Everything. Sit down, and listen. The scaffold they are building won't be for Fantômas.

FANTÔMAS: What are you saying?

MARQUISE: That you will soon be free.

FANTÔMAS: Oh, Madame, the house is guarded and in less than two hours—

MARQUISE: The impossible doesn't exist for Fantômas—and in less than two hours, you will be free!

FANTÔMAS: Explain yourself!

MARQUISE: It's all child's play. Listen. When the doctor that admitted you said you weren't dead, and had you transferred to the prison infirmary, they took me to the woman's prison. From there, by means of money, cunning and help from our companions, I was able to escape. I placed myself at the head of the gang. Everything's the same, the treasury in my power, the associates more faithful than ever. Fantômas always triumphs—here and everywhere.

FANTÔMAS: Continue!

MARQUISE: I was present, disguised at your trial—thinking of ways to save you. I couldn't think of any, but the Devil opened a way for us. The great actor, Leonard Emmanuel of the Comédie Française, was present as I was at the trial, studying you great care and attention, so as to portray you in a drama that was staged two nights ago, with Emmanuel playing a criminal soon to be executed; he supplanted you on stage, succeeding in an enormous escape, assuming your face, your dress, your gesture.

FANTÔMAS: Continue.

MARQUISE: Emmanuel is in love, and a womanizer. The women raffle him off, write to him, make trysts with him. They are capricious, and one of them wrote to him giving him a rendezvous for tonight, between one and two in the morning, but on the condition that he come dressed and made up exactly as he was represented in the papers and as he appeared in the applauded drama.

FANTÔMAS: Enough! I understand! You were that lady. If he comes, he falls into the trap. He will be seen to enter; but I'll be the one to leave.

MARQUISE: It won't be quite like that. The house we are in was bought a month ago. Also purchased was the house in the rear which backs on it and which is entered from a parallel street. The two houses have been joined—by means of drilling by our favorably disposed friends.

FANTÔMAS: You are worthy of me, I recognize it.

(The masked Fantômas and others enter from the armoire.)

MARQUISE: What's up?

MASKED FANTÔMAS: Coming around the corner, a man dressed in a magnificent fur over-coat, with a broad hat covering his head—

MARQUISE: No doubt it's Emmanuel—the man that we are waiting for—that Number Four received with all sorts of details. Bring him here immediately.

MASKED FANTÔMAS: You will be obeyed.

(He exits.)

MARQUISE: You see, fortune favors us. In a short time Fantômas will be free! Come!

FANTÔMAS: I will obey you. You are worth of being obeyed.

MARQUISE: Go in here, you'll only have to wait a short time.

(Fantômas goes into a side room. Pause. After a short time, Margot emerges from the armoire leading Emmanuel dressed as Fantômas.)

MARGOT (leading Emmanuel in): Take care, my gentleman. There's a small step here—there it is. Very good. Allow me to take your hat and overcoat. That's it.

The blindfold won't leave you until the lady who's waiting for you orders arrives.

EMMANUEL: I'll obey with all my heart and soul, beautiful child.

MARGOT: Then goodbye and good luck. May happiness await you!

(Margot leaves by the way she came. The Marquise appears, face covered with a mask.)

MARQUISE: You may take the blindfold off now, sir.

(Emmanuel removes the blindfold; they both look at each other.)

EMMANUEL: What a superb boudoir! Can you remove your mask, Madame? I don't understand—

MARQUISE: It's my fancy! I see that you are punctual and compliant.

EMMANUEL: Madame, I always am. You desired that I come here this way, and thus I come to you as I am on stage. Believe that—

MARQUISE: I will reveal myself soon, my dear. After following your performances, I wanted to spend the night with Fantômas.

EMMANUEL: Then, Fantômas I shall be! Reveal yourself at least, my beauty.

MARQUISE (unmasking): Here I am.

EMMANUEL: Oh, delightful.

(He hugs her.)

MARQUISE: Dinner is waiting. Later we will have plenty of time.

EMMANUEL: To dine seems to me just the thing. Afterwards—

MARQUISE: Afterwards, eternity. The eternity of pleasure that is in my arms.

EMMANUEL: For your beauty, for your eyes—

(raising a glass of Champagne to the Marquise, he drinks it; they sit facing each other.)

MARQUISE: You've got an appetite. I want Fantômas.

EMMANUEL: An enormous appetite, my beloved.

MARQUISE: Call me, Marquise.

EMMANUEL: Glad to, my beloved Marquise. An enormous appetite for your beauty—for your irresistible eyes.

MARQUISE: Jesus! You are terrible!

EMMANUEL: What do you want—so much time in prison, ha, ha— (laughing) Distance from the delightful ladies, my fierce criminal instincts, ha, ha!—bring out passionate desires, ha, ha!

MARQUISE: Very well, thus, I'm going to sate your desires.

EMMANUEL: The truth is, Madame, that you are extremely capricious and your capriciousness reduces me so much. You don't love me as Emmanuel, the great actor, you love me as—

MARQUISE: As Fantômas! That's right, and you must keep your look, your type, to please me. To possess me, you must possess me as Fantômas!

EMMANUEL: That's somewhat hard.

MARQUISE: If it doesn't seem good to you, we can call my maid, who will blindfold you and later—

EMMANUEL: Later, they will put me out the door—me. No, this adventure still seems like an enchantment to me. Fantômas or Emmanuel, Emmanuel or Fantômas, either way, I am the most wholehearted admirer of your beauty.

MARQUISE: That's what I want to see. (giving him a cup of Sherry) To our night of love.

EMMANUEL: To our night together! (drinking) Do you know, beloved Marquise, that your wine is delightful. Where does it come from?

MARQUISE: It's Sherry—Spanish wine.

EMMANUEL: You are the most beautiful—

MARQUISE: That's the wine talking.

EMMANUEL: Don't you believe it, Madame. With or without wine, there's no doubt about it, you are enchanting. My God!

MARQUISE: What's up?

EMMANUEL: How this devilish wine goes to my head!

MARQUISE: Bah! You cannot drink.

EMMANUEL: That would be to declare myself conquered, and neither in wine, nor in love, am I ever vanquished.

MARQUISEL Bravo! Those words are worthy of Fantômas.

EMMANUEL: How like him I am! For these eyes, for this face, I'm capable of robbing the bank of England, of murdering you, if you don't fall in my arms, mad with love; surrender before my eyes.

(He tries to stand up but cannot)

EMMANUEL: No—running off, idolized woman, you cannot change your dwelling.

MARQUISE: Maybe you're seasick?

EMMANUEL: Me, seasick, me? Ha, ha! There's no wine in London sufficient to make me seasick. Your eyes, your eyes are what intimidate me; what intrigue me. Long live your eyes, Marquise! Marquise of what? What are you the Marquise of, ha, ha, ha!

(There are three knocks on the door.)

MARQUISE (aside): They've come for him. (to Regarden, outside) Be with you in a minute.

(going to open; she puts on her mask before opening the door. Regarden and the two guards enter.)

REGARDEN: Time is up.

MARQUISE: I know it. Here, take him.

(She leaves. Regarden comes forward.)

EMMANUEL: Hey, who's this lean and ugly man. Ha, ha—what a bandit's face.

REGARDEN: Plainly, dinner was good.

EMMANUEL: Where are you taking me? Where did you come from anyway? Who are you? Ha, ha—what a stupid face. And where's the Marquise?

REGARDEN: The Marquise? Let's go. The wine's had an effect. Better that way, you'll feel it less. Come, friend Fantômas, the hour has come.

EMMANUEL: The hour for what?

REGARDEN: To return to your cell.

EMMANUEL: To my cell? Ha, ha. Where's the Marquise? Let them take me to the Marquise.

REGARDEN: Let's go. The wine has knocked him out and we're going to have to carry him.

FIRST GUARD: Better. That will make him more depressed.

EMMANUEL: Eh? Who might you be? Why are you grabbing me.

FIRST GUARD: Let's go, Fantômas, let's go. We're wasting time.

EMMANUEL: But where are we going? Are you crazy?

REGARDEN: Where are we going to go? Why, to lock you up again and prepare you for the ceremony.

EMMANUEL: The ceremony?

REGARDEN: Fine. Enough nonsense. Move!

SECOND GUARD: Let's go, Fantômas.

EMMANUEL: Fantômas—hey? I'm not Fantômas! You are making a mistake. Let me go.

(they start to pull him)

EMMANUEL: I am not Fantômas, I am—ha, ha wine, Spanish wine. Thanks to it, I no longer know who I am. Ha, ha, ha, but I know for sure, dear friends, who I am not. That I am not Fantômas. Ha, ha—I am not Fantômas.

(He resists helplessly, they carry him off—he can be heard protesting and the guards laughing as they vanish. Pause.)

MARQUISE: Fantômas.

FANTÔMAS (emerging): Thank you, Marquise.

MARQUISE: You will be free! Look! (taking him to the balcony) They're carrying him to the scaffold.

FANTÔMAS: He seems to be resisting.

MARQUISE: It doesn't matter! Be calm. Yonder is Fantômas!

BOTH: Ha, ha, ha!

MARQUISE: Let's not waste time.

(She goes to the armoire, opens it; Margot and the masked Fantômas enter.)

MARQUISE: It's over. I promised it. Here is our chief.

ALL: Long live Fantômas!

FANTÔMAS: Thank you, my friends! Thus you see, with us, with The Thirteen, with Fantômas, nothing is impossible. With one foot on the scaffold, Fantômas disappears, and someone else takes his place. We are powerful, and the world is ours.

(goes to the balcony)

FANTÔMAS: Will you look at the stupid masses who come to see me die, my last gesture. Imbeciles, they are looking at someone else's last gesture, and Fantômas turns in struggle! Tremble and wait, stupid masses. Fantômas didn't die!

MARQUISE: Everything's ready. A nine-horsepower auto awaits us at the corner. Inside, you'll have what is necessary to transform yourself. (to Margot) Hoods?

MARGOT: That of Madame la Marquise and mine are already in the auto.

MARQUISE: Very good. Our companions?

MASKED FANTÔMAS: Waiting for us in the cellars at Frances Road.

MARQUISE: You will dress as a chauffeur?

MASKED FANTÔMAS: In the adjoining house. I also carry the passports and credit letters drawn on several major international banks.

FANTÔMAS: Hurrah! Never was any monarch better served. Thank you! Fantômas is yours!

MASKED FANTÔMAS: And we belong to Fantômas!

MARQUISE: Let's go!

FANTÔMAS: Without losing a minute. Thirteen?

ALL (with enthusiasm): Here and everywhere!

CURTAIN

ACT II

Same as Act I. AT RISE, the stage is dark, the only light comes from a hanging lamp.

(A tumult of voices can be heard. Juez, Ruy, Regarden and the same two guards enter.)

JUEZ: Lights! Lights! Quick! (to Regarden) It was here?

REGARDEN: Yes, here!

JUEZ: Fine. Search this house. And the adjoining one. (The Warden starts to go) You told us too late!

REGARDEN: Sir!

JUEZ: Mr. Ruy, did you inform Inspector Juve?

RUY: Yes. I advised him immediately by telephone.

REGARDEN (emerging): There's nothing anywhere!

JUEZ: What wretches you are! Mr. Ruy, cuff these men! (Ruy handcuffs Regarden and the two guards.)

REGARDEN: Mr. Juez! Please!

JUEZ: Not a word! (to Ruy) Mr. Ruy, bring up some chairs and make these three swine sit. (Regarden and the guards are forced into chairs.)

JUEZ: Now tie their feet!

RUY (does so): Done!

JUEZ: There! You three, shut up! We will wait for Inspector Juve on the landing. The sight of these rascals makes me sick. Let's go. Come with me and lock the door behind you, Mr. Ruy.

RUY: As you direct.

JUEZ (looking at the three prisoners): You will stay here until Inspector Juve arrives.

REGARDEN: But Mr. Juez—

FIRST GUARD: Mr. Juez—

JUEZ: He will decide what's to be done with you. Good bye.

(Juez and Ruy leave, locking the door behind them. A Pause.)

FIRST GUARD: We are prisoners.

SECOND GUARD: We are lost.

REGARDEN: Our poor heads!

FIRST GUARD: What will become of my poor wife?

SECOND GUARD: And my poor mother.

REGARDEN : And my children.

FIRST GUARD: I told you this business would be very dangerous.

REGARDEN: That's very true. But 500,000 pounds are not to be ignored.

FIRST GUARD: We will lose them.

REGARDEN: As to that, no. I have them in a safe place, and when our isolation is over, I'll get in touch with my sons. They will distribute them between our three families religiously. At least they will have a secure life.

FIRST GUARD: And what, my God, about ours?

REGARDEN: What's to be done now? Life in the penitentiary, I expect. A thousand sunbeams. If Fantômas were to see us—what would he say? For serving him, we end up like this!

FIRST GUARD: Maybe he would help us?

SECOND GUARD: Maybe he would save us?

REGARDEN: Yes. And maybe I'm the King of Spain!

(The armoire opens. Fantômas, the Marquise wearing her mask and another Masked Fantômas appear.)

FANTÔMAS: Onto your side!

MARQUISE (to each one): On your side!

ALL THREE (frightened): Hey!

FANTÔMAS: Silence!

(The guards are untied and the handcuffs removed.)

138

FIRST GUARD: Thanks!

SECOND GUARD: Thank you!

REGARDEN: Sir, you may dispose of us!

FANTÔMAS: Be free! This way leads to the street; at the corner, there's an auto—in it are another 500,000 pounds. Pick up your families and go to France or wherever you like. But fast!

ALL THREE: Long live Fantômas!

FANTÔMAS: Be on your way now—and silence!

(The three guards leave through the armoire.)

FANTÔMAS: Now, put out the lights and let's each take a seat, gun in hand.

MARQUISE: The situation is going to be funny.

FANTÔMAS (to the Masked Fantômas): Put it out.

(He does. The stage becomes dark. A pause. On the landing, on the other side of the door)

JUEZ: Open the door, Mr. Ruy. I changed my mind. We'll take the statements of these disgraceful people.

(Ruy and Juez enter.)

JUEZ: Hey, what's this? Who put out the lights? Come on, Mr. Ruy! Turn the lights on!

(As the lights come on, the two men are confronted by Fantômas, with a revolver pointed at them.)

JUEZ: Holy Trinity!

RUY: Blessed Saint Barbara!

MARQUISE: Not a word, not a gesture!

JUEZ: But—

RUY: I—

MARQUISE (pointing her weapon): Silence! The handcuffs!

JUEZ: On who? On me?

MARQUISE: You first! Sit down!

(Ruy obeys.)

MARQUISE: Come on, I'm in a hurry!

(Juez sits. First she cuffs him, then Ruy.)

MARQUISE: Very well. You look very nice. How amusing you are! Have a nice night!

(They douse the lights and leave by the armoire.)

RUY: Nice situation, beloved Commissioner.

JUEZ: You'll never see me in one like this again.

RUY: We're lucky we escaped with our lives.

JUEZ: Would they be that bold?

RUY: I think so.

JUEZ: We ought to be able to get out. They left our feet free.

RUY: But if we move, they can with one shot turn our brains to dust.

JUEZ: How barbarous! But they are very capable of it.

(Sounds from the landing.)

JUEZ: Ah, to get it over with—Here comes Juve!

JUVE (off): Where is Mr. Juez?

POLICEMAN: Inside, Mr. Juve.

(Juve and the Police Officer enter.)

JUVE (amazed): Why—what happened here? What is this?

JUEZ: You see, friend Juve. It was the bandits.

JUVE: Which ones?

JUEZ: Fantômas and his gang.

(Juve and the officers untie the two men, then the officers leave.)

JUVE: I am at your service, Mr. Juez—what happened?

JUEZ: A trifle. A foolish thing. (pause) Fantômas has disappeared.

JUVE: What?

JUEZ: Fantômas has evaporated.

JUVE: But how can that be so?

JUEZ: I'm going to tell you. It seems that the gentlemen at the prison, giving in to great influence or great donations, or maybe both, brought Fantômas here to spend the final hours of his life in the arms of a woman, whom they believed was his lover. At the agreed hour they brought him here.

JUVE: And he escaped?

JUEZ: Not quite! But they left him, and when they came back to get him, they picked up another man, a drunk, but his clothes, his face, his maniacal gestures, everything indicated that he was Fantômas—despite his protests. They grabbed him and carried him back to the prison and incarcerated him in his cell. We got there a little later. We came to interrogate him one last time before taking him to the scaffold. Despite his dreadful condition, he told us that he wasn't Fantômas, and before our astonished and surprised eyes, he tore off his beard and mustache, cleaned himself rapidly with his own clothes, and we were all in the greatest stupor—his face matched that of the great actor, Leonard Emmanuel, of the Comedie Française.

JUVE: What are you saying? I'm not sleeping?

JUEZ: No, Juve, we are all perfectly wide awake.

JUVE: Then—

JUEZ: Then the thing is perfectly clear. Fantômas entered here, and from here Leonard Emmanuel emerged. Interrogated rapidly by me, he was only able to get out phrases about a nearby house, a dinner, a Marquise, Spanish wine, and falling down due to the effects of the powerful narcotic they had given him

JUVE: And nothing more?

JUEZ: We also found this invitation making the rendez-vous, and insisting that he wears the clothes and make up in which we found him.

JUVE: That explains the substitution perfectly. Oh, he's admirable! What a genius of invention—quite wonderful.

JUEZ: Yes. The idea is extraordinary.

RUY: Of the first order.

JUVE: And afterwards?

JUEZ: Afterwards, the Warden and two prison guards disappeared.

JUVE: You let them escape?

JUEZ: Oh, no, they evaporated as if by enchantment. We'd brought them here and tied them up, hand and foot, and left them here, locking the door behind us—planning to wait on the landing. I found the presence of those two scalawags disturbing. But later, it occurred to me that, while waiting for you, we should get a statement from them. We entered this room—

RUY: And found it dark.

JUEZ: And when the lights went on, we were met by three masked individuals, revolvers in hand, threatening us. They forced us to sit in these chairs the way you found us.

JUVE (unable to contain himself): Ha, ha, ha. I owe you thanks, many thanks.

RUY: I told you he'd laugh at us.

JUVE: Pardon me, Mr. Juez.

JUEZ: No—Yes—I , too, would laugh at myself. Notwithstanding, don't make me curse mercy. It was a real lesson. We don't need another.

JUVE: The thing that has to be done now is to catch these criminals soon as possible.

JUEZ: Certainly.

JUVE: Did you search this house?

JUEZ: I did, but without finding anything.

JUVE: Those three masked individuals were not the prison guards and the warden, right?

JUEZ: No—those t had disappeared. The three masked individuals were dressed in tights. And one of them was a woman.

JUVE: I see! Fantômas and two of his companions. You weren't able to see where they went?

JUEZ: I didn't see a thing.

JUVE: What about you. Mr. Ruy?

RUY: It was impossible to see because they left the room in the dark.

JUVE: You didn't hear the noise of some door?

JUEZ: Absolutely nothing.

JUVE: Nothing has been changed from its place in this room?

JUEZ: Nothing has been touched.

JUVE: All right! Let's proceed. A splendid dinner was set here for two. Let's see— (seizing the glasses) From this one, nothing was drunk. Without doubt, it was the glass of a woman and one who didn't want to drink. The other drank champagne and sherry wine in abundance. Mostly, sherry wine. (sniffing the bottle) Ah, the Devil—I know that narcotic—I've used it many times. Mr. Ruy, keep this bottle. (giving Ruy the bottle of Sherry) Is the actor Emmanuel in condition to make a statement?

JUEZ: According to the prison doctor, he'll sleep for around ten hours.

JUVE: A much shorter sleep than the one they destined for him. (meditative pause) This house undoubtedly has another hidden entrance. There's not the least doubt. And it's in this room. This room is the end of that secret passage. Let's look at the bed. (raising the mattress) No, it's an ordinary bed—it's not there. Let's look at the rest... Ah, prepare yourself to be astonished. Mr. Ruy, take your revolver in hand and be on alert. If anything strange happens, if Fantômas and his men return, or turn out the lights and disappear into thin air—don't hesitate—shoot!

RUY(obeying): That's what I'll do.

JUVE (to Juez): Now we can search calmly.

JUEZ: Mr. Ruy, point that gun at the ceiling. You're making me nervous. But stay here and don't go rushing off somewhere.

RUY: Yes, boss.

JUVE: With your permission, Mr. Juez, I—just in case—brought my own revolver—

(taking his revolver and going to the other door.)

JUEZ: Yes, yes, of course. Every precaution is needed with these people. We'll see about looking now.

(Suddenly, the light goes out and two Masked Men emerge from the armoire, put a hood over Juez's head and take him away. Ruy fires his gun, but at the ceiling.)

RUY: Mr. Juve! Come back! Quick.

JUVE: What happened?

RUY: Mr. Juez has disappeared!

JUVE: Damn! This is getting complicated. But from where do these people get in and get out? (Pause; looks around) Ah, yes, of course! The armoire!

RUY: Let's hurry to rescue Mr. Juez. Don't lose any time. I am burning with desire to find a clue. The scandal is going to be tremendous.

(Juve goes to armoire and opens it. At the back is a card. Juve reads it in an altered voice)

JUVE: Eh! This paper... Number Thirteen with a question mark after it. "My dear Juve, I carried off Mr. Juez, who is a remarkable man. You, my friend, need to rest. That is absolutely indispensable to me. I need twenty-four hours in order to save myself from your clever investigations. If you are quiet, Mr. Juez will be returned safe and sound to his home. If not, he will disappear forever. Remember me to the Minister. Bye, bye, friend Juve—Ever yours, Fantômas."

RUY: What can we do?

JUVE: Nothing. It would be completely useless.

RUY: Then we should leave here immediately.

JUVE: Hold on a minute. Maybe the sound of my voice will reach Fantômas. (in an altered voice) I accept your conditions, Fantômas! I'll rest for twenty-four hours, but as soon as the first minute of the 25th hour strikes, I'll be hot on your trail again. I swear not to rest until I'm able to raise from the shining blade of the guillotine the infamous head of Fantômas.

CURTAIN

ACT III

Three years have passed.
A beautiful room in the home of the Italian ambassador. It is night. Electric chandeliers. Four doors. At the back, a balustrade. Guests are dressed as diplomats from many nations. The Duke de Mirandela is dressed as a Colonel from some Italian Regiment. A number of people surround him and applaud as he finishes speaking.

ALL: Bravo! Bravo for the Duke!

PRINCE CROSTANDY: Beloved brother, receive my most enthusiastic congratulations for your glorious adventures.

PRINCESS CROSTANDY: By God, gentlemen, let me blush for the poor man.

DUKE DE MIRANDELA: May you all receive my most expressive gratitude. But it's not worth all this trouble.

PRINCESS CROSTANDY: It would be nothing, but I want, in front of everyone, and with the permission of my husband, the Lord Ambassador—and in the name of all Italy—to give you my reward.

DUKE DE MIRANDELA: Beloved sister!

PRINCESS: This hug.

PRINCE: I don't want to do less.

(The Prince hugs him, too.)

FIRST GUEST: Gentleman, a Hurrah for the Duke de Mirandela.

ALL: Hurrah!

PRINCESS CROSTANDY: I cannot tell my beloved brother, the brave soldier returning from the field—that he will not be received with all honors.

DUKE DE MIRANDELA: Oh, for God's sake!

PRINCESS CROSTANDY: No: to the dining room. Here, with casks of Champagne—let us save them in order to make you happy. (to the Duke) Come, brother.

DUKE DE MIRANDELA: En route.

PRINCESS CROSTANDY: Hail to the Duke of Mirandela!

ALL: Hail!

(They leave. Pause. After a bit, the Marquise de Grantley appears, dressed all in black. She enters very cautiously. Then she signals to someone in the garden that it is safe to enter. One hears the sound of a waltz from the adjoining rooms. A Masked Fantômas enters. Calmly, both the Fantômas and the Marquise go into an adjoining room. A Pause. Then the Duke returns, arm in arm with Minister Gamer.)

GAMER: No doubt, you, my dear Duke. All that was said is exact. During the time you were out of the country, many things occurred here. An infinity of things—quite memorable.

DUKE DE MIRANDELA: You leave me astonished. You can't still believe that this devilish personality—Fantômas—is anything but the child of popular fantasy?

GAMER: Popular fantasy, eh? No! He's the son of the very Devil!

DUKE DE MIRANDELA: A cigarette?

GAMER: Ah, yes—thank you!—before the ladies latch on to us and deprive us of it. Let's use these moments that we have alone.

(The Duke gives Gamer a cigarette. They light up.)

DUKE DE MIRANDELA: By what means did Fantômas escape?

GAMER (his speech and thoughts become slurred): By playing a trick on Juve that took the fight out of him.

DUKE DE MIRANDELA: Truly?

GAMER: Nothing less than taking possession of Police Commissioner Juez and keeping him hostage until he was safely returned.

DUKE DE MIRANDELA: How daring.

GAMER: Bah! It was marvelously effective.

(The narcotic in the cigarette begins to take effect.)

DUKE DE MIRANDELA: And when did all this happen?

GAMER: Approximately three years ago.

DUKE DE MIRANDELA: And the detective?

GAMER: Juve has sworn to find Fantômas and deliver him to the guillotine.

(He falls into a lethargy. Pause. The Duke gets up and looks around, goes to the door and says to in a low voice.)

DUKE DE MIRANDELA: Thirteen?

MARQUISE (she opens a door): Here and everywhere!

DUKE DE MIRANDELA: Bravo! Where is Number 11?

MARQUISE: Here, inside, putting on his makeup.

DUKE DE MIRANDELA: Let's go!

(They carry Minister Gamer into the room.)

MARQUISE: The plan of your brother's dwelling?

(She laughs.)

DUKE DE MIRANDELA: Silence! Don't be crazy! Here it is!

(He gives it to her.)

MARQUISE: Very good. You can be calm. Your orders will be carried out to the letter. Don't separate yourself for a moment from the Prince and the Princess.

DUKE DE MIRANDELA: What about the false Gamer?

FALSE GAMER (emerging from the side room dressed exactly as Minister Gamer.): Present!

DUKE DE MIRANDELA: Perfect! Obeyed like this, Fantômas will always be great.

MARQUISE: Thirteen?

BOTH: Here and everywhere!

(The Marquise leaves. The False Gamer and the Duke de Mirandela sit together as before.)

DUKE DE MIRANDELA(as if continuing a conversation): Ha, ha—your stories are admirable.

FALSE GAMER: I swear to you it's all true.

PRINCESS CROSTANDY (entering): But what are you doing here all alone?

DUKE DE MIRANDELA: Dear sister, we wanted to smoke a cigarette in peace and so we shut ourselves up here.

PRINCE CROSTANDY (following her): Well done! With your permission, I am coming to do exactly the same thing.

PRINCESS CROSTANDY: Men! You are incorrigible!

DUKE DE MIRANDELA: Bah! General excuses—you may return to the salon, dear sister.

PRINCESS CROSTANDY: Ah—but what about you?

DUKE DE MIRANDELA: I am famished. Let's leave the Lord Ambassador and Minister Gamer—who dedicate themselves calmly to puff smoke.

PRINCESS CROSTANDY: I agree with you, dear brother. How does that strike you, friend Gamer?

FALSE GAMER: That he talks like a book.

(She leaves with the Duke, The Prince sits down.)

PRINCE CROSTANDY: Jokes, friend Gamer. Weigh them and don't make them. In place of a cigarette, we will smoke a superb Havana. How do you like that?

FALSE GAMER: Now that's a princely idea.

(The Prince rings a bell. An usher enters in grand livery.)

PRINCE CROSTANDY: Havanas!

USHER: Those Your Highness smokes?

PRINCE CROSTANDY: Yes. Bring one of those boxes over my bed. Would you like to play a game of chess, Minister?

FALSE GAMER: With great pleasure.

PRINCE CROSTANDY: You heard.

USHER: At once.

PRINCE CROSTANDY: Tell me, Minister, how do you like our brave Duke de Mirandela?

FALSE GAMER: Who's returned after almost three years transformed into a soldier.

PRINCE CROSTANDY: For some time, we thought him dead. So, when we received notices from the Minister of War that he was alive, and he was going to be given a leave of absence—this house where he's adored enjoyed a moment filled with crazy happiness.

FALSE GAMER: He seems very nice.

PRINCE CROSTANDY: I've got a plan to attach him to the embassy and find a wife for him.

FALSE GAMER: You couldn't have a better plan.

PRINCE CROSTANDY: It's not a bad one. There are always opportunities.

USHER(returning): The chess set and the Havanas, Your Highness.

PRINCE CROSTANDY: Very good. You may withdraw.

(They set up their chess pieces, smoke, and begin to play.)

FALSE GAMER: No, Prince, no. Check by the Bishop leaves a way out. I am stronger.

PRINCE CROSTANDY: Bravo! I like having a worthy adversary.

(reaction by False Gamer)

PRINCE CROSTANDY: What's wrong?

FALSE GAMER: I don't know I felt faint. It's nothing.
To the queen.
(playing)
PRINCE CROSTANDY: Oh, you are bold! What am I
holding this knight for?
(The Marquise appears with an air-powered rifle. She is
masked.)
FALSE GAMER: And me this Bishop?
PRINCE CROSTANDY: Never mind. Checkmate in
four moves.
(The False Gamer seems to collapse. The Prince rises to
help him.)
PRINCE CROSTANDY: But what's wrong, friend
Gamer?
(The Prince has his back to the balustrade. The Marquise
aims at him and fires. There is no sound because she is
using her air-gun.)
PRINCE CROSTANDY: My God! (grabbing his shoul-
der) I'm dying!
(He collapses.)
FALSE GAMER (rising slowly): Well done.
MARQUISE: The bullet—find the bullet!
FALSE GAMER: Here it is.
MARQUISE: Now the other one. Let's go!
(They go to the side room. They return with the uncon-
scious Gamer and place him in the seat across from the
one in which the cadaver of the Prince is slumped. Then
the Marquise and the False Gamer leave. Pause. From
the other direction, the guests, led by the Duke and the
Princess, enter. Juve and Sir Erdeval, the Minister of
Justice, are among them.)
PRINCESS CROSTANDY: This way, gentlemen. Seize
these incorrigible smokers, and bring them to the salon,
too.

JUVE: I'll take advantage of this moment to pay my respects to the ambassador.

PRINCESS CROSTANDY: Look here. Why, they are both asleep. What does it look like to you?

ALL(laughing): Ha, ha, ha.

DUKE DE MIRANDELA: They are feigning. And we are being deceived.

PRINCESS CROSTANDY: Mr. Ambassador—Minister—enough joking.

DUKE DE MIRANDELA: Mr. Gamer—enough of this farce.

(reaction)

GAMER (awakening): Eh? Who? What's going on?

(amazed)

ALL: Ha, ha!

GAMER: Was I sleeping?

(getting to his feet)

GAMER: I beg your pardon—But?

PRINCESS CROSTANDY (to her husband): Come on, Mr. Ambassador! Wake up—you, too!

(Silence)

PRINCESS CROSTANDY: Fernando. Come on! (softly) Enough of this.

DUKE DE MIRANDELA: Wake up, my dear brother. The comedy is over.

(Juve observes the Prince.)

JUVE: One moment, Milord. (pause) Mr. Gamer—don't leave the house. (to the Duke) Take your sister away. The Prince is dead.

DUKE DE MIRANDELA (stunned): What are you saying?

JUVE: That Prince Crostandy is dead.

PRINCESS CROSTANDY: My God! Is it true? Fernado! My Fernando!

(weeps and hugs him)

JUVE: Mr. Gamer—be so good as to explain yourself—tell us what happened here?

GAMER: That attitude—this question?

JUVE: It's the question of the law. The friend has disappeared, the guest too—now, I am only the detective. Minister Gamer, you must answer me.

ERDEVAL (to Gamer): please answer.

GAMER: Of course. You can question me when you please!

JUVE: When we came in, were you actually sleeping or feigning to be asleep?

GAMER (indignant): Why—?

JUVE (energetically): Were you sleeping or feigning?

GAMER: I was really sleeping.

JUVE: And how do you explain it?

GAMER: I don't know. The Lord Duke and I—we came here with the idea of smoking a cigarette—isn't that right?

DUKE DE MIRANDELA: That is correct.

GAMER: After a while, I felt seized by an unconquerable desire to sleep.

JUVE: Right. Doped—isn't that right?

GAMER: I don't know—what I know is I felt profoundly sleepy—here—where the Prince is seated.

PRINCESS CROSTANDY: Mr. Juve, the Minister is lying—with unheard of boldness.

GAMER: Princess!

PRINCESS: I repeat—lying! Hardly were you here, sir, when the Duke came to this salon with my husband and I. As you know, my brother and I returned to the dining room—and we left the Prince here with you, Mr. Gamer—and, at the time, you were perfectly awake.

DUKE DE MIRANDELA: The Princess spoke the truth.

GAMER (energetically): Milord Duke!

DUKE DE MIRANDELA (energetically): Mr. Gamer!

JUVE: Here's a chess set and a box of Havanas. And on the floor—half a smoked cigar.

GAMER: I didn't smoke any cigars.

JUVE: What do you mean, you didn't? (he rings bell, the Usher and other servants enter.) Find out who brought this chess set here—and this box?

USHER: I did, by order of His Highness.

JUVE: Very good. Who was here? Was His Highness alone?

USHER: No, sir—there was also this gentleman.

JUVE: Sleeping?

USHER (surprised): No, sir, awake.

JUVE: You may withdraw.

(The Usher and the other servants leave.)

JUVE: I have trouble understanding you, Mr. Gamer. Your attitude and your negativity.

ERDEVAL: My dear colleague, be so kind as to talk. Your position is all too obscure and is compromising the investigation.

GAMER: What are you saying?'

JUVE: I'm saying that we found a dead person here—possibly dead of a violent death. That the companion of this person was you, and that you don't know or don't wish to explain to us absolutely anything of what took place.

GAMER: Because I know absolutely nothing.

JUVE: We will soon know—Doctor Gramendi was at the dinner just now. Let's beg him to come here. I request all of you, until the arrival of the Doctor, to observe the most profound silence. He mustn't know anything of what has occurred. Princess, hide your tears for a moment.

154

FIRST GUEST: Here comes the Doctor.

DOCTOR GRAMENDI: What's happened, my friends. Who has fallen ill?

JUVE: It seems that His Highness Prince Crostandy has passed away. We would like you to examine the body.

DOCTOR GRAMENDI (examining him): My God! What's this? Gentlemen! (pause) The Prince is dead.

JUVE: Doctor, can you tell us how he died?

DOCTOR (examining the body): Yes. There's no doubt. The Prince died of a bullet to his heart. Here, in his uniform, is the entry wound of the projectile.

JUVE: Mr. Gamer—what do you say to this?

GAMER: I say, Mr. Juve, that I don't know a thing— and that I find your bold questions in very bad taste.

JUVE: In the near future a judge will ask you to reply.

GAMER: What?

JUVE (to Sir Erdeval): Minister, I ask for the permission to arrest Mr. Gamer, in the name of the law.

ERDEVAL: Gamer, you heard him. You are under arrest.

GAMER: Me? I'm a prisoner?

ERDEVAL: And at the disposal of the police until this matter is cleared up.

DOCTOR GRAMENDI: It would be suitable to move the Prince to another room where I can make a more careful examination.

JUVE: Do it!

(The Usher and several servants carry the Prince's body to another room, followed by the Princess.)

GAMER: I swear to all of you, gentlemen, I am completely innocent of all this business.

ERDEVAL We really hope so.

JUVE (thoughtfully): Mr. Gamer—did you bring any weapon with you?

GAMER: Nothing, I brought nothing. If you doubt it, search me.

JUVE: We shall! Were you separated from the Prince at any time?

GAMER: I repeat to you and to all, that I wasn't with the Prince and that I was with the Duke.

DUKE DE MIRANDELA: My dear friend, it's certain that you were with me, but afterwards, the Prince and the Princess came—you were left alone with the Prince. My sister and I withdrew and I went to the dining room. Everyone knows it—am I right, gentlemen?

FIRST GUEST: And all together, we came in search of you and the Ambassador.

GAMER: You are going to drive me crazy if you don't stop!

JUVE: Mr. Gamer, you cannot deny the evidence. I myself accompanied the Duke and his sister into the dining room. And then I came here with them. How can you persist in claiming that you were with the Lord Duke?

GAMER: You can weigh it all; I swear that what I said is true.

JUVE: I regret with all my heart the evil road this business is going to take.

DOCTOR GRAMENDI (returning): Mr. Juve—Gentlemen, I have to inform you all that I must modify my previous statement.

JUVE: Speak, Doctor!

DOCTOR: I can assure you that His Highness the Prince was killed by a steel bullet—that went through his back, and exited his chest. The bullet piercing his heart came from a weapon that didn't use conventional ammunition.

JUVE: What! There was no conventional ammunition employed? Is that what you just said?

DOCTOR GRAMENDI: Without a thread of doubt.

JUVE: A compressed air gun, right?

DOCTOR GRAMENDI: That's it!

JUVE: And how long ago?

DOCTOR GRAMENDI: Approximately an hour.

JUVE: Ah, Fantômas, Fantômas! Again we meet! Mr. Gamer, you didn't kill the Prince, but you were the accomplice of his murderer.

GAMER: Me!

JUVE: Yes, indubitably, you helped make it possible. (Pause) Milord Duke, be so kind as to sit in the Prince's seat. Mr. Gamer, sit where you were.

(They do.)

JUVE: Place yourself in the attitude of playing chess. Like thus! The Prince took the bullet in his back. The place here is in the line where the assassin was. Exactly—in that room. Whose room was it?

DUKE DE MIRANDELA: It's a room that leads to other rooms.

JUVE: Whose?

DUKE DE MIRANDELA: To the rooms that were designated as mine.

JUVE: Will you permit me to search them?

DUKE DE MIRANDELA: With all my heart, Mr. Juve!

JUVE: Thank you. Stay in the same position that I put you; now change.

(Pause)

ERDEVAL: I supplicate you once more, friend Gamer, to say what you know about what I presume that led to this terrible crime.

(Gamer remains silent.)

ERDEVAL: Again this obstinate silence! But don't be afraid—the justice that I represent places you under its protection and shelter.

GAMER: I maintain what I said. That's all there is.

(Juve gets up slowly, and pulls his revolver, which he points at the Duke, who doesn't see him, but Gamer does.)

GAMER: What are you doing, Mr. Juve?

JUVE: Investigating what role you played in the killing of the Prince. The same way I see you now, you saw the murderer of the Prince. Oh, what a suspicion! Mr. Gamer, swear to me on your mother's grave that it's certain you were under the influence of a powerful narcotic.

GAMER (solemnly): I do so swear.

JUVE: Sir Erdeval—your colleague is innocent. Yes—I am beginning to see clearly. I've got all the clues now. You are free, Mr. Gamer—but on the condition of helping me, of helping justice clear this up. We will proceed calmly. After leaving you here with the Prince, what happened! Speak your mind—by your sainted mother!

GAMER: I don't know. After being with the Duke for a while, I lost my reason, I slept, that I know—and I woke up only when you all came—I swear it.

JUVE: Then you were under the control of a superior power—such as hypnosis.

GAMER: It's very possible.

JUVE (to the Duke): You don't notice anything in all this?

DUKE DE MIRANDELA: Absolutely nothing.

JUVE: Let's think—the bullet. We've got to find this bullet... What I mean, Milord, is this—if you were facing the Prince, why didn't the bullet kill you, too? Let's see. Sit here—like this... No—not like that. Ah, he was here—but higher. He got up, that's it. You may stand up, Milord Duke. You stay seated, Mr. Gamer. Let's see. That's it. That's it, precisely. (to the others) The Prince was standing when he was killed. You, Mr. Garner, were sitting, or lying on the table at the time, lethargic.

There's no doubt about it. Ah, Marquise de Grantley, once again you used your diabolical rifle.

(Noise. Raised voices.)

ERDEVAL: What's going on? What uproar is that?

PRINCESS CROSTANDY: What's happening, my God? What new misfortune?

(Emilia, the Princess's elegantly dressed chamber maid, enters.)

JUVE: What occurred! Talk fast!

EMILIA: What happened is that, while going to the Princess's room, I saw with horror, that all the armoires, all the drawers, had been forced open—all were completely empty.

PRINCESS CROSTANDY: Robbed!

ERDEVAL: How brazen!

ALL: What audacity!

ERDEVAL: This is too much.

JUVE: Actually—it is unimportant. This robbery was meant to confuse me. It's a much bigger thing that we hold in our hands. It's necessary that the Princess authorize me to come and go, and remain in her palace as long as I deem it necessary.

PRINCESS CROSTANDY: As of this moment, and in everyone's presence, I authorize you—

JUVE: Thank you, Madame. Mr. Gamer and you. Milord Duke, also offer me their agreement, right?

DUKE DE MIRANDELA: With life and soul!

GAMER: With true enthusiasm.

JUVE: Then I pledge this—the game is going to begin, and this time, I swear to you that Fantômas and his terrible gang will very soon be checkmated.

CURTAIN

ACT IV

An office in the palace of the Italian embassy. There is a large desk near a balcony and a door leading to the bedroom of the Princess, an entrance door, and another door on the opposite side. It is Night. Doctor Gramendi, Juve, and the Duke de Mirandela enter from the Princess's room.

DOCTOR GRAMENDI: It is very distressing, but I think it a sacred duty to speak openly.

DUKE DE MIRANDELA: You have us on pins and needles, Doctor.

JUVE: Yes. Speak and be quick about it.

DOCTOR GRAMENDI: Very well then. I think the illness of the Princess, whose origin lacks importance, has undoubtedly something strange about it. It has worsened in a noticeable way; it is destroying the effects of the medicine, and, if left to itself, may imperil her life.

DUKE DE MIRANDELA: What are you trying to say?

JUVE: Speak clearly.

DOCTOR GRAMENDI: In this palace, there's a criminal hand furnishing a poison to the Princes—a poison I am unfamiliar with, but whose alarming progress I see clearly.

BOTH: A poison!

DOCTOR GRAMENDI: Without the least doubt.

DUKE DE MIRANDELA: But that is impossible.

JUVE: For Fantômas, nothing is impossible.

DUKE DE MIRANDELA: So you believe—?

JUVE: Yes, I believe it all. This good Doctor, most of all. As of today, the Duke and I will take turns at the bedside of the patient. Is that what you desire?

DOCTOR GRAMENDI: Yes—it's the only way that my medications will be administered, and the only way to ensure that no one poisons the Princess.

JUVE: Meanwhile, I'll take it upon myself to discover and cut off this criminal hand that you denounced to us.

DUKE DE MIRANDELA: Oh, thanks, friend Juve.

JUVE: I'm only fulfilling my duty.

DOCTOR GRAMENDI: With your permission I'm going to see my patient. You can accompany me if you like.

JUVE: You go, Milord, and remain on guard until I relieve you. Let's begin this very hour.

DUKE DE MIRANDELA: Excellent idea! Let's go.

(The Doctor and the Duke leave.)

JUVE: I am in one of the most difficult moments of my life. Events are tossing me about, and I cannot yet find the thread that will lead me to the truth.

RUY(appears, dressed in livery): May I come in?

JUVE: Come in! What do you want?

RUY: To talk with my boss.

JUVE: Your boss?

RUY: Yes, boss. The same one who ordered me to stay around so as to be around if needed.

JUVE(recognizing him): Ah, Officer Ruy!

RUY: In the palace, and at your service. I took the place of a servant that was fired and completed four days without losing sight or sound or observation.

JUVE: And what else?

RUY: Something—and very serious.

JUVE: Eh? Don't be slow to say it.

(He checks the doors to see if anyone is there)

JUVE: And that door ? (points to a third door) It doesn't concern you?

RUY: That door has been locked with a key for the last three days.

JUVE: How do you know?

RUY: This door communicates with a passageway that leads to the salon where the Prince was killed.

JUVE: It's true. Continue.

RUY: In that salon, there's a balustrade, this balustrade from the garden—and the garden—

JUVE: Get to the point.

RUY: In the garden last night, between three and four in the morning, two persons were talking—mysteriously— one was a lady dressed in black and wearing a mask.

JUVE(stunned): The Marquise de Grantley!

RUY: Yes, the Marquise.

JUVE: And the other? Who was the other?

RUY: The Duke de Mirandela!

JUVE: Are you crazy?

RUY: No. It was the Duke.

JUVE: Ruy, that's impossible. Watch what you say.

RUY: The lady has a key to this door. She enters the garden and leaves by the balustrade. She crosses the salon. Afterwards, this room. She comes and goes here. A bit later, she wants to leave, accompanied by the Duke. This took place on two of the four nights I was on watch.

JUVE: You got a good look at the Duke?

RUY: As I see you. The nights were very clear.

JUVE: Not a word, not a gesture that can denounce you. And keep watching without rest.

RUY: Trust me. I'll watch!

(Ruy salutes and leaves silently.)

JUVE: The thread is getting tangled. Could what Ruy says be true? Soon I'll be free of doubts.

(He leaves. Pause. Then the door Ruy said has been locked for three days opens and the Marquise enters, followed by two Masked Fantômases, both with revolvers in hand. She goes straight to the desk. But it is locked. Hearing a noise, they retreat and leave quietly.)

DOCTOR GRAMANDI (entering with the Duke): She sees much calmer, Milord, but, above all, don't leave the Princess alone, even for a minute. Meanwhile, I will prepare the medication, and only you, or Juve, or I, will administer it to the Princess.

DUKE DE MIRANDELA: Thank you!

DOCTOR GRAMANDI: In this way, and only in this way, can I answer for the life of your sister.

DUKE DE MIRANDELA: I'll accompany you, Doctor.

DOCTOR GRAMANDI: I'll come back tonight.

DUKE GRAMANDI: Until then.

(The Doctor leaves.)

DUKE DE MIRANDELA (alone): This stupid Doctor has screwed us up completely. What are we going to do now? It's going to be necessary to stop for a while—right now. But what about Juve? I must get him out of here on some pretext. Ah, yes. The telephone. Magnificent idea. (dials) Central? Communication with 60-50-9. Yes. (looking around) Let's be sure no one can observe. (goes to door) No one there. (responds to bell ring.) Ah, speaking. Yes, it's me. 13?—The Marquise is not there. That's OK. Call the Police Headquarters. Demand the presence of Juve at some place far from here.—You understand? Fine. Let five minutes pass. Bye. (putting down the phone) Now, to take care of my sister in the place of Juve.

(The Duke leaves. Ruy, who has been eavesdropping, enters.)

RUY: Get Mr. Juve far from here? It seems to me that it's not going to be possible, my dear Duke. For great illnesses, great remedies.

(rings a bell)

USHER (entering): You called?

RUY: Yes. Ask Mr. Juve to come immediately. He's called to the telephone. This is the room of the Princess. I cannot leave her.

USHER: Willingly.

(He leaves.)

RUY (meditating a bit): Now, to wager all.

(He cuts the phone wires.)

JUVE (enters): Headquarters called me?

RUY: Yes, sir.

JUVE (taking the phone): The line is dead. It doesn't answer.

RUY: I cut the cables.

JUVE: What? Have you gone crazy?

RUY: Not at all. We must confuse the Duke. Tell him you have to leave immediately on an urgent case. Take this key. Exit to the street. Turn at the corner, and return by the service door. The last door on the corridor is my room. Once there, don't say anything. Go, find it. This goes to the life of the Princess.

JUVE: Understood! Give me the key.

(Ruy puts the key in Juve's outstretched hand. Silently they leave in different directions. Pause. Then Ruy returns with a Notary.)

NOTARY: Be so kind as to inform the Princess and the Duke of my arrival.

RUY: With great pleasure.

NOTARY: It's five to four. I imagine we'll be soon finished.

RUY(announcing): Milord the Duke de Mirandela.

DUKE: My dear Mr. de Samay!

NOTARY: I am at the orders of Milord Duke and your sister, the Princess Crostandy.

DUKE DE MIRANDELA: She is Much improved from her sorrows.

NOTARY: My congratulations. I imagine that my presence is required for—

DUKE DE MIRANDELA: It's about the opening of my dear brother's will.

NOTARY: I see. What about the Princess?

DUKE DE MIRANDELA: As she is in a delicate condition, she has appointed me.

NOTARY: Very well. What is indispensable are two witnesses.

DUKE DE MIRANDELA: Could Inspector Juve be one?

NOTARY: I should say so! And as for the other—any of your servants will do.

DUKE DE MIRANDELA (rings, Ruy enters): Ask Mr. Juve to come in a minute.

(Ruy leaves.)

NOTARY: The will?

DUKE DE MIRANDELA: Here it is. Take it.

RUY (announcing): Inspector Juve.

DUKE DE MIRANDELA: Friend Juve—I have to beg you the favor of a few minutes prior to your leaving for Police Headquarters.

JUVE: Sure, if it's not much.

NOTARY: I'll delay you only for the time necessary to open and read this will.

JUVE: Fine.

DUKE DE MIRANDELA (to Ruy): You remain, too; you will serve as witness.

RUY: I am at your service.

DUKE DE MIRANDELA: Then, my dear Notary, when you please. Sit here.

NOTARY: "In the City of London, etc., etc., etc." Here we are: "I appoint, by the present testament, my universal heir to of all my wealth—without exception—my beloved spouse, Magdalena, Princess de Crostandy. It is also my absolute will that, in the event of my beloved spouse failing to survive me—that all my wealth, without exception, go to my beloved brother, the Duke of Mirandela."

RUY and JUVE: Ah!

NOTARY: The rest is boilerplate. There's the signature, and the seals. Everything seems to be in order. Do you have more to add, Milord Duke?

DUKE DE MIRANDELA: Absolutely nothing.

NOTARY: I've brought the act of opening. It only lacks the signature of you and the two witnesses. Here, Milord.

(The Duke signs.)

NOTARY: Now you, Mr. Juve.

(Juve signs.)

NOTARY: Now the servant.

(Ruy signs.)

NOTARY: Very good. In the morning I'll bring the deed to all the property that will be placed at the disposition of the Princess.

DUKE DE MIRANDELA: Whenever you please.

NOTARY: Milord Duke, Mr. Juve—always at your service.

(The Notary leaves.)

JUVE: Do you want anything else?

DUKE DE MIRANDELA: I owe you a million thanks, and leave you at liberty to rush to Police Headquarters.

JUVE: What about your sister?

DUKE DE MIRANDELA: I won't leave her for a moment.

JUVE: I'll return as soon as I can.

DUKE DE MIRANDELA: When you do, you will be well received.

(The Duke accompanies Juve as he leaves. Then the Dukes laughs and leaves as well. Pause. After a short time, Juve and Ruy quietly return.)

JUVE: Friend Ruy, it's not necessary to tell me anything I don't already know. I've guessed it all.

RUY: I thought so.

JUVE: Don't lose sight of the Duke for a second. And be ready for anything.

RUY: I shall be.

JUVE: Do you know what I saw when I signed the deed?

RUY: What?

JUVE: I saw the handwriting of Fantômas!

(Ruy is stunned. Juve falls silent.)

CURTAIN

ACT V.

The same as Act IV. Night. The stage is lit by the chandelier at the center of the room.

DUKE DE MIRANDELA: This cursed servant has signified to me, with all due respect, that until he receives orders from Juve, he won't leave the room of the Princess, even for a moment. To insist on vexing him would only give rise to terrible suspicions. Bah! Better then to stay here. No danger of any surprises. The hour is approaching. The Marquise ought not to be late. Let's see. Nothing. Silence and sleep on all sides—
(two raps)
DUKE DE MIRANDELA: That's her. Enter.
(goes to door)
MARQUISE: Here I am. Did Juve leave?
DUKE DE MIRANDELA: He did. Where's Number 11?
MARQUISE: In the garden, watching my retreat.
DUKE DE MIRANDELA: In that case we can talk calmly.
MARQUISE: I think so, too.
DUKE DE MIRANDELA: It's necessary to finish things tonight.
MARQUISE: Then we'll finish them.
DUKE DE MIRANDELA: But Juve's ordered one of the servants not to leave the side of the Princess for anything.
MARQUISE: Magnificent! This one's going to be the scapegoat—the murderer.
DUKE DE MIRANDELA: It's always a pleasure to listen to you, from the first word. All right—but I cannot

168

figure a way of getting the poison served in front of this headstrong servant.

MARQUISE: Yes, that's tricky. (pause) Ah, that's how! Sit down and write.

DUKE DE MIRANDELA: Dictate.

MARQUISE: "To Number 10, by order of Number 13." That's to be on the envelope.

DUKE DE MIRANDELA (writing): It's there.

MARQUISE: Now the letter. "Without losing a moment, impregnate a letter—ordered and signed by Juve—with the most powerful narcotic that we have. And send it to this address: To the servant who is guarding the Princess.—By order of Juve."

DUKE DE MIRANDELA: Of Juve. Done.

MARQUISE: Sign and send the letter.

DUKE DE MIRANDELA (does so): Take it.

MARQUISE: Bring it.

(Takes it to the balcony, opens it, and flashes a light. Pause.)

MARQUISE: He sees it. Answers with his. Fine. That brings it closer. Now, I'll drop the letter in the garden.

(She tosses the letter.)

MARQUISE: And in half an hour, it will be delivered by an associate disguised as a policeman, and when the servant reads it, he'll go into a deep sleep whether he wants to or not.

DUKE DE MIRANDELA: When will he wake?

MARQUISE: The Princess will die and will hold in her pockets the proof of his crime.

DUKE DE MIRANDELA: Exactly.

MARQUISE: Another thing. In the plans of this palace you gave me, and that I have been studying—there's a clearly marked subterranean and secret passage—which begins at the bank of the river Thames and ends precisely in this office.

DUKE DE MIRANDELA: What are you saying?

MARQUISE: We need to carefully study this room to see if there's some sort of spring—it would almost be child's play.

(She looks at the wall, as does the Duke, both looking for a hidden spring. Then three knocks.)

DUKE DE MIRANDELA: Could that be Number 11?

MARQUISE: No—he's been ordered not to abandon his post.

DUKE DE MIRANDELA: Hide here—behind this door. (loud) Who is it?

JUVE (outside): It's me. Open up, Milord.

DUKE DE MIRANDELA: It's Juve! (aloud) What's it all about?

JUVE: Good evening. I was unable to come earlier.

DUKE DE MIRANDELA: Earlier? Why?

JUVE: Why? I entered this place very simply. I opened the garden gate. Once in, I jumped to the balustrade of the salon—crossed through the passageway and here I am.

DUKE DE MIRANDELA: And could you explain why you did this to me?

JUVE: It's very simple. I wanted to convince myself if someone could get in here—where you are now—and now I'm convinced.

DUKE DE MIRANDELA (alarmed): Of what?

JUVE: Besides, this way, no one but you knows of my arrival.

DUKE DE MIRANDELA: But if I hadn't been here—?

JUVE: I counted on luck! Naturally, the Princess is sleeping, the servant, carrying out my orders hasn't abandoned her, and you came here for a moment to smoke, to write, to breathe some air, and you see that I wasn't fooled, the balcony was open.

DUKE DE MIRANDELA: You are admirable.

JUVE: Do me a favor, Milord. Permit me to smoke. Would you like a cigarette?

DUKE DE MIRANDELA: No, thank you. And why did you return so—?

JUVE: So quickly, right? Because I never left.

DUKE DE MIRANDELA (pale): What?

JUVE: Upon leaving here, I thought, maybe it was a false alert—to get me away from here—so I decided not to go. I sent a message to Police Headquarters that I was too busy.

DUKE DE MIRANDELA: Very well done.

JUVE: Are you are really completely of my opinion? I hope so. The most lamentable thing, Milord, is that it bored me enormously to come here—because—because I made several rounds of the park without discovering anything.

DUKE DE MIRANDELA (aside): I breathe easier. (aloud) What were you expecting?

JUVE: To discover something. For example—an open balcony. Like, for example—

DUKE DE MIRANDELY (aside): He's seen her!

JUVE: —A compressed air rifle. In the end, I didn't want to trouble you, Milord. Now that I'm here—I'll relieve the servant, and you can withdraw and get some sleep. When you please—I'll remain here.

DUKE DE MIRANDELA (alarmed): Here?

JUVE (calmly): Here, yes, in this office. It's a better place to watch the Princess. In case the servant whom I told to inform me of any news needs me—because through here is the only entrance to the rooms of the Princess—so here I'll stay.

DUKE DE MIRANDELA: But—and if—

JUVE: Don't worry about a thing, Milord. I am armed and I am not sleepy.

DUKE DE MIRANDELA: The fact is—I am a little sleepy.

JUVE: There you are! It's so nice of you to want to keep me company. No, no—I won't permit it. You need sleep.

DUKE DE MIRANDELA: But...

JUVE: Not at all, not at all, Milord Duke. Till tomorrow. (rings bell; Usher enters.)

JUVE: Accompany the Duke to his room.

DUKE DE MIRANDELA (aside): I have no remedy. (aloud) Then—until tomorrow, Juve.

JUVE: Sleep tight.

(The Duke leaves with the Usher.)

JUVE (aloud): I'm going to do my daily report, and after that, I'll relieve the servant—the poor fellow must have a craving to go to bed.

(Juve smiles and lights a cigarette, then checks his revolver to see if it is loaded. Pause)

MARQUISE (aside): Cursed Juve! How do I get out of this mousetrap? (pause) Suppose I venture out?

(Juve is pretending to write. The more deeply absorbed he seems, the further she advances. He stops writing, she stops. Then he appears to start again, and she advances. Abruptly, Juve stands up.)

JUVE: A very nice night, Madame la Marquise.

(She stops stupefied and goes for her revolver.)

JUVE: What's this? Did I frighten you?

(no reply)

JUVE: Silence is useless. Through your mask, I know you, Madame la Marquise.

MARQUISE: Well, then—yes, it is I! (removing her mask)

JUVE: I tolerate no revolver but my own. You do enough with your marvelous rifle.

MARQUISE: Mr. Juve, I'm not in a joking mood. Seize me if you can, and get it over with.

JUVE: No—first I need to catch your accomplices. And Fantômas, of course.

MARQUISE: Fantômas is far away from here. I'm working for myself.

JUVE: Congratulations. And in that case—how's business?

MARQUISE : Fine. And yours—does it go well?

JUVE: Mine? Ah, my dear Marquise. Mine *is* yours.

MARQUISE: I don't understand.

JUVE: That's too much! In the end, my dear Marquise— before delivering you to my officers—you'll do me the favor of telling me where Fantômas is.

MARQUISE: I'm unaware of it.

JUVE: But I'm not.

MARQUISE: Then why ask me?

JUVE: Like me, you know that Fantômas is very close.

MARQUISE (illuminated by an idea): That's very possible. Maybe closer than you think

JUVE (rattled): What?

MARQUISE (as if speaking to someone behind him): Kill, Fantômas, kill!

(Juve turns quickly and, almost as quickly, she escapes by a side door.)

JUVE: Ah, imbecile—I fell for it like a fool. Was I born yesterday?

(goes to door)

JUVE: Clumsy of me to leave it open. Now, there must be some way to catch her. Juve, my friend, you are in the most ridiculous situation. (calling) Ruy! Ruy!

RUY (entering): What happened?

JUVE: Nothing, my boy. I just lost a battle. The Princess?

RUY: Sleeping peacefully.

JUVE: Then run to Police Headquarters. Get Commissioner Juez to come. And bring a squad of policemen to surround the house.

RUY: If you want, I can reconnect the telephone wires.

JUVE: You're right. That would be quicker.

(Ruy reconnects the wires and calls and gets an answer.)

JUVE: Central—Police Headquarters—thank you. (to Ruy) She slipped through my hands.

RUY: Who?

JUVE: The Marquise. (into the telephone) It's me, Inspector Juve. I need Commissioner Juez to come to the Italian Embassy right away. Also a squad to watch the Embassy in every direction. And to detain suspects. Fine. Fine—Goodbye. (to Ruy) Are you sleepy?

RUY: No, sir.

JUVE: Good. In ten minutes you are going to receive a letter from me. I need you to sleep as soon as you have opened it. Understand?

RUY: Perfectly.

JUVE: Then return to your post once—and pretend as if nothing has happened.

(Ruy leaves.)

JUVE: Demon of a Marquise. I wasn't played badly. Ah, but I'll catch her. And I will revenge myself. Eh? What's that? Ah, Duke—

DUKE DE MIRANDELA (returning): Friend Juve, pardon me; it's impossible to sleep. I'm worried.

JUVE (meaningfully): I believe you. I, too, am nervous. I'm beginning to be plagued by a bad headache—but fortunately—

DUKE DE MIRANDELA (aside): But where can the Marquise be?

JUVE (after having heard something): There—I heard it.

DUKE DE MIRANDELA: What?

JUVE: It's like I heard the pain inside my head.

DUKE DE MIRANDELA: Ah, then you can be glad that—

JUVE: Yes, but I don't know if a cigarette or something—I'm as sort of dazed—I'd like to go out for a minute to get some air.

DUKE DE MIRANDELA: If you like, I will stay here on guard.

JUVE: Thank you. I was going to suggest it. So—abusing your friendliness, I'm going to take a turn in the garden. I'll be back soon. The Princess—

DUKE DE MIRANDELA: Go ahead—don't worry.

(Juve leaves. The Duke quickly goes to the door.)

DUKE DE MIRANDELA: Locked. Yes. She escaped and Juve must not know about it. Here's the report Juve was writing—making good use of the moment, she got away—Ah, what a load off my mind.

USHER: With the Lord Duke's permission.

DUKE DE MIRANDELA: What's going on?

USHER: They've just brought this letter for the servant who is in the Princess's room.

DUKE DE MIRANDELA: Fine—you can deliver it.

(The Usher goes into the Princess's room.)

DUKE DE MIRANDELA: Courage, Fantômas. In a short while, the servant will be sleeping deeply. Then—it's your game.

(The Usher returns and leaves.)

DUKE DE MIRANDELA: Let's see. (Looking out the balcony) Yes—there is Juve walking about peacefully.

(going to another door) This door is very well locked. So let's remove this door latch. (going to the door of the Princess) And here—the servant struggling with sleep.

Now's the time. Everyone asleep here. (to Ruy) Are you asleep yet? (no response) Within ten minutes, you will have increased the treasury of our association by four million pounds.

(He goes into the room of the Princess. As soon as he does, Juve jumps over the balcony.)

JUVE: Commissioner Juez—I'll be with you in a moment.

(Juez enters. Then Juve and the go into the Princess's room. After a short pause, they return holding the Duke.)

DUKE DE MIRANDELA: I don't understand this, gentlemen, the reason for this insult. It is unworthy. (to Juez) Who are you?

JUVE: This is Police Commissioner Juez. Now, have the goodness to tell them what type of medication this is, which you were about to drop in the medicine of the Princess just as we got there. Do you know you are caught in flagrante delicto of poisoning?

DUKE DE MIRANDELA: False! This—this flask contains a new medication ordered by the Doctor in your absence.

JUVE: I had the pleasure of introducing you to Commissioner Juez. Now, I'm going to have no less pleasure in doing the same with Doctor Gramendi.

(Doctor Gramendi enters.)

DOCTOR GRAMENDI: That is a lie.

JUVE: Gentlemen, I have the immense pleasure of presenting to you Duke de Guerin, the poisoner of the Princess Crostandy, the organizer of the murder of Prince Crostandy, the thief of the identity of Duke de

Mirandela, the convict escaped from the scaffold. In a word, our old acquaintance—Fantômas.

DUKE DE MIRANDELA: This man is crazy, this man lies!

JUVE: You escaped from prison, then became involved in the war, I know—there you made friends with the authentic Duke de Mirandela, you were companions in arms; in the midst of combat, the Duke died. You didn't kill him—but I believe that your brain rapidly formed the idea of taking his place in society. Rapidly you discarded your former identity and appropriated his. The same height, the same build, almost the same situation. All the documents of the Duke in your power. But around there were injured persons who witnessed all this without being able to stop you. They later died in ambulances but first signed a report of your actions. Of this report I'll have a copy in my hands tonight...

DUKE DE MIRANDELA: No one will believe you.

JUVE: Fantômas, all this is useless. You cannot escape. You yourself locked this door; now I'm going to go to you and get the key that you have in your power.

DUKE DE MIRANDELA: Me?

JUVE (with energy): Give me that key.

DUKE DE MIRANDELA (giving it): This is an insult.

JUVE: It's doing justice. Very good—now, it's impossible to leave except by the balcony. I've got two agents below, with orders to blow the brains out of anyone trying to jump out. As for this door—you know that no one can escape that way. As for this one, the Commissioner has placed himself in front of it, revolver in hand. You see, Fantômas—you will go from here directly to the guillotine—which clamors for you. Remove your mask and confess to Mr. Juez and to me your identity, and all your crimes. There's no other remedy.

DUKE DE MIRANDELA: Very well. Yes, I am Fantômas.

JUVE: Bravo!

FANTÔMAS: But if you came thinking to see me tremble—you are mistaken. I am Fantômas—I'll say it again.

JUVE: With great pleasure. Give me your elegant hands. (places cuffs on them)

FANTÔMAS: Here they are. Fasten them tight. So they don't find a way to your throat.

JUVE: Thanks for the warning, but I'm not concerned. Mr. Juez, for the second time, I deliver Fantômas to you.

RUY (entering, excited): Mr. Juve, Mr. Juez!

JUVE: What's up?

JUEZ: What's going on?

RUY: A stupendous thing.

JUVE: Get to the point!

RUY: When I separated the curtains of the bed to give medicine to the Princess—

JUVE: Well?

RUY: The bed was empty. The Princess had vanished.

(Rapidly Juve, and the others rush to the room of the Princess leaving Fantômas alone. From behind the desk the Marquise emerges.)

FANTÔMAS: I am lost.

MARQUISE: Not yet.

(removing the cuffs)

FANTÔMAS: You?

MARQUISE: The subterranean passage has two entrances in this palace. One, in the Princess's quarters and the other one, here. Let's go.

(Fantômas follows the Marquise into a trap door located behind the desk)

FANTÔMAS: Ha! Ha! See you, Juve! Let's go.

(He closes the trapdoor behind them.)

178

JUVE: Wretch! Do you know where the Princess is? And Fantômas?

JUEZ (running from door to door; all are locked): And the Duke?

JUVE: Mr. Commissioner—and Fantômas?

JUEZ: I don't know. There's no exit here.

(Juve checks the doors, baffled)

JUVE: Or here either. But which way did these people disappear?

JUEZ: I have to admit this man is miraculous.

JUVE: Unfortunately for humanity! Vanquished! Foiled again by Fantômas!

C U R T A I N

ARSÈNE LUPIN VS. SHERLOCK HOLMES: THE HOLLOW NEEDLE

Inspired by Maurice Leblanc's novel
By Heraclio S. Viteri and Enrique Grimau del Mauro
(1912)

CHARACTERS

Elena de Thibermesnil
Laura de Saint Veran
Henrietta
Horace Velmont / Luis Valmeras / Arsène Lupin
Georges de Thibermesnil
Abbé Gelis
Inspector Ganimard
Isidore Beautrelet
Jeannot
Gomel
A Servant
Various Policemen, Lupin's gang members

ACT I

A Gothic room in the Chateau de Thibermesnil. It is richly furnished. On one side at the back there is a monumental library in 2 parts separated by a large bracket with the name "Thibermesnil" in relief. There is also a glass showcase with containing various artistic objects including a book with a red velvet cover.

AT RISE, Georges de Thibermesnil, Abbé Gelis, and Horace Velmont are involved in a discussion.

GEORGES (continuing the conversation): What you told them surprised them, really? The famous thief has surprised me in a very eloquent fashion.

VELMONT (gravely): That's a bad sign.

ABBÉ: And how did this Lupin announce his visit?

GEORGES: Three days ago, I picked up a book in this library. Here is the book and here is the hollow of the second page—

VELMONT: Then Arsène Lupin was here?

GEORGES: Indubitably.

ABBÉ: But—was it Lupin—and no other—who made this, er, withdrawal?

VELMONT (affirming): Who else?

GEORGES: But why only this book? I don't see what Lupin could get from it—profitably, I mean.

VELMONT (laughing): Dear Georges! Let me laugh over your situation.

GEORGES: As you please, Velmont. But don't laugh at Abbé Gelis, who is very erudite in historical matters, especially when the stolen book is *The Chronicle of Thibermesnil*. What importance it can have to that thief, I'm unable to say.

ABBÉ: I understand perfectly: This precious chronicle of the 10th century is consecrated in its entirety to narrating the precious deeds of your ancestors—it contains a description of a secret subterranean tunnel—

VELMONT: A tunnel?

GEORGES: We are unaware where its entrance is, but we know it exists. All I know—and this is from tradition—is that its entrance is in the field, and its exit is in this dwelling.

VELMONT (laughing): Then knowing it, it provides an easy solution. All one has to do is to search the whole castle.

GEORGES (interrupting): There's nothing easy about it, friend Velmont, nothing at all. My ancestors, for a century—and I, too—one after the other, tried to locate this invisible entrance. You know how, in the Middle Ages, they made these things. Everyone knows there is a secret entrance that opens in this wing—but no one knows where it is located. In what plane of the wall, in what flagstone of the pavement, is the solution of the problem to be found? What mysterious spring, what little button hidden from sight, should be pressed or uniquely twisted to open the unknown passage in the wall. Before what stone, before what ornament, before what relief in this antique dwelling shall we say the words "open sesame" of the fairy tales?

VELMONT: In effect, if the book says no more than that, it will be of little use to the thief. What a disappointment to have carried it off.

ABBÉ: Who knows? After all the marvelous adventures we hear of this man—or rather, devil incarnate! The stolen book provides in various places provides a very imperfect record—like plans of the tunnel—and these plans could well be useful.

GEORGES: Impossible. These plans throw no light on the underground entrances, and much less the way to open invisible entrances that none mention. In short, these plans can be used to know the form of the tunnel and its approximate location—but nothing more. I've looked at them a hundred times and I wanted to use them myself. I made excavations and yet—nothing. A mysterious success occurred in the middle of the 18th century by a member of my family who died in some war without being able to communicate it to his successor.

VELMONT: You can rejoice that Lupin appears to have made a useless robbery.

GEORGES: Completely useless. And if he is vigorously seeking to find an entrance into my chateau through this subterranean tunnel—I pity him. Don't you feel the same?

ABBÉ: Me? I agree—it is impossible from the mere study of these plans to do so, but in conjunction with the legends that I've repeated to you many times—

GEORGES: You, Abbé, have too much love for these legends—as a historian and collector of rare inscriptions—and obstinately seek in each of them some impossible explanations.

VELMONT (intrigued): And what legends are these?

GEORGES: Two ancient monuments that contain much to be seen in the history of our kings. But nothing to do with secret entrances to the underground.

ABBÉ (a bit annoyed): You are forgetting that these clandestine amours took place in this chateau, and that our kings utilized these tunnels.

VELMONT (with interest): Let's hear these legends.

ABBÉ: One of them is very short. It says only, Thibermesnil 2-6-12.

VELMONT: Hum! That sounds like a multiplication: 2 x 6=12.

GEORGES: Quite right. Thank you!

VELMONT: Let's hear the other.

ABBÉ: What it says might make us laugh.

GEORGES: It's a childish thing. But go ahead, say it.

VELMONT: Yes, please.

ABBÉ: No—my friend Georges is making it into a joke.

GEORGES: I shall repeat it as I heard it from you fifty times, since you don't want to humor Velmont.

ABBÉ: I'll do it for him, but don't laugh. Listen, this is the inscription: "The axe swings—

GEORGES (with comic seriousness): The axe flies—

ABBÉ: —In the trembling air—

GEORGES: Or the shivering breeze.

ABBE: —And the ell opens and one journeys towards God."

GEORGES: Or goes straight to God. So what? Do you still link this bit of verse to the secret tunnel entrances, Abbé?

VELMONT (aside) Imbecile! I believe it does provide the solution. (aloud, laughing) Congratulations for telling it to us, Abbé.

ABBÉ: Are you laughing, too? Fine! I'm confident in my belief that this legend contains the key to the problem. Sooner or later it will be deciphered, and—

GEORGES (unable to stop laughing): Abbé, for the love of God, I can't—I can't stop laughing—

VELMONT (aside): Idiot! (aloud) And does our friend Lupin know of this inscription?

GEORGES (ironic): Fortunately, I don't believe so. Imagine if he knew it.

ABBÉ (sententiously): Perhaps he does. And you will deplore it, my friend.

ELENA (entering, a small package in her hand): Georges, they just brought this—

GEORGES: On whose behalf?

ELENA: Our cousin, Stephen.

GEORGES: Ah, I know what it is. The notebooks he promised me yesterday.

(He places the package without opening it on the table.)

ELENA: Georges, with the permission of these gentle-men—

(Georges and Elena speak apart)

GEORGES: And who brought them here?

ELENA: It's in your dispatch. Laura has come too.

GEORGES: Well, she'll be satisfied to be in such good company.

ELENA: Yes, she's in her room, changing clothes.

GEORGES (turning to the Abbé and Velmont): Gentle-men, I'm going to give you some news. As of this mo-ment, two guests have arrived, who are preparing a noc-turnal surprise for this thief, Lupin. Inspector Ganimard, the famous policeman who once captured him, and a young apprentice, detective by inclination, who gives signs of emulating the celebrated Sherlock Holmes.

ABBÉ: I see that you are well prepared.

GEORGES: Solely, to calm my wife.

ELENA: Who really needs it. A month in continuous uproar! And it's to someone like this Lupin that we owe it.

ABBÉ: Then you can rest easy now.

VELMONT: These preparations you've taken are not bad, Georges, because I suppose that the young appren-tice you've just spoken of is—Isidore Beautrelet.

GEORGES: The same.

VELMONT: All things considered, I don't think that Ganimard and Beautrelet are enough to stop Lupin in his triumphant career. Wouldn't it be better to call Sherlock Holmes himself?

GEORGES: You said it, Velmont. And he, too, has been called at the urging of my wife.

ABBÉ: And is he coming?

GEORGES: This very night. At midnight he will come to the Chateau de Thibermesnil. As of tonight, the king of detectives will be our guest here. See this telegram.

(He pulls a telegram from the package and gives it to Velmont.)

VELMONT (aside): Sherlock Holmes, here! (aloud, reading) "Coming—ferry 11:40 p.m." (smiling) Congratulations, Georges!

ABBÉ: Indeed, you can sleep safely.

ELENA: I think so. Thanks to God. We need a bit of tranquility.

GEORGES: With your permission, I am going to show these gentlemen around. And you, Elena, while I'm with our friends, watch over Laura.

VELMONT: Laura?

GEORGES: A relative of mine I brought here. Laura de Saint Veran; a sweet young thing that I commend to you, friend Velmont.

VELMONT (aside) She, here! (he seems visibly vexed.)

GEORGES: Gentlemen, till shortly.

(He leaves with his wife.)

ABBÉ: Good-bye, Georges. (Noticing Velmont's attitude) You look thoughtful, Velmont?

VELMONT (dissimulating) I was thinking about what Georges revealed to us. Sherlock Holmes is coming to capture Lupin. He says that he needs his help—as if all the police in France are not enough, we need also help from England. What a great man this Lupin must be!

ABBÉ: Don't speak foolishly, Velmont. He's simply a thief—no matter how clever he may be.

VELMONT: England against France. The astute Briton against the cleverness of France. And who will win?

ABBÉ: Lupin will fall—inevitably.

VELMONT (energetically): Who knows? He's such an extraordinary man.

ABBÉ: However extraordinary he may be, he'll be defeated. Men as extraordinary as he will persecute him—Sherlock Holmes, Ganimard, Beautrelet.

VELMONT: That's not a bad trinity to overcome him. But I'm sure he'll do the best he can with them. (changing tone) Changing subjects, you who are so erudite, and an aficionado of history, have you ever heard of the secret of the Man in the Iron Mask?

ABBÉ: You mean, the secret of the Hollow Needle?

VELMONT: Yes, of this strong lair supposedly located in this region, that remains a mystery to all the world, except for the throne of France—a fortified tower that hid fabulous treasures—a mystery that cost the life of Joan of Arc, the infamous an in the Iron Mask, Captain Laberge—

ABBÉ: My dear Velmont—this is another secret like that of the entrance to the tunnel of Thibermesnil. Except that, in the mystery of the Hollow Needle, there are two unknowns. Everyone is ignorant of the place where this natural refuge exists, and the means to take it. The last member of the royal house that possessed this secret was Queen Marie Antoinette, who had it written on a parchment that Louis XVI sent to her before dying by an officer of the Royal Guard. And this parchment contained—or so I'm told—a mysterious inscription consisting only of points and signs, and in the final line, a hieroglyph which is supposed to contain precise instructions for finding the Hollow Needle.

VELMONT (with interest): And this inscription, this parchment—where is it?

ABBÉ: It's lost. I've read about it in a pamphlet that said that Marie Antoinette sent it in a book of devotions to

Count Fersen before leaving for the scaffold. But I don't believe it—because a book of devotions contains no hiding place and, moreover, this devotional is here in this library. I've seen many things in it, but not that inscription. It has, on its first page, a dedicatory sentence written by the Queen in her own blood to Fersen. The authenticity of the book is indubitable.

VELMONT (going to the showcase): So then—this book is the devotional! O bloody relic! And with what veneration I contemplate you. What's certain is that in little more than a century many great, magnificent, curious things have been lost.

ABBÉ (assenting): The lack of curiosity of men defeats some, kills others. The prodigies of our times have been wasted.

(Georges enters with Ganimard and Beautrelet.)

GEORGES: Gentlemen, I'm going to present to you Inspector Ganimard of the Sûreté and Monsieur Isidore Beautrelet. Abbé Gelis—my best friend—and Horace Velmont, an incomparable artist in pastels.

VELMONT: I really wanted to meet you both. The newspapers have mentioned your names many times—more than once in conjunction with Arsène Lupin.

GANIMARD: Phooey! Let's talk of other things—

BEAUTRELET: This time, there won't be much of a fight. We've got the thread that will lead us to him.

VELMONT (aside): Idiot!

ABBÉ: God grant that it may be so.

GEORGES: I'm sure they will get him.

VELMONT (ironic): Are you of the same opinion, Mr. Ganimard?

GANIMARD: I affirm that we will find him out.

VELMONT: You heard him, Georges—will you allow me to examine the notebooks that your cousin sent you?

GEORGES: With a thousand pleasures. They are magnificent, I think they are by Rubens. (untying the package) You will see, Velmont, if indeed— (suddenly disconcerted) It's my book—the stolen chronicle!

ABBÉ (approaching): But—

VELMONT: What cynicism!

GANIMARD: Arsène Lupin is like that—he steals and boasts of the robbery. But this time—

GEORGES (finding a card in the leaves of the book): Here's a card. (reading) "My dear sir, I have the honor to return to you this precious chronicle. Keep it carefully, because it is a jewel of the art of typography, and pardon me for having borrowed it for a few days. I no longer need it. Please accept this testimony of my appreciation—Arsène Lupin."

VELMONT: Is he bold!

BEAUTRELET (ironic): Ah, we have a complete thief there.

ABBÉ (indignant): And one that no one is able to put a hand on.

BEAUTRELET: He'll be free for a short while longer—but there's not much time left for him.

GANIMARD: A few hours, no more! (waving his fists threateningly) Ah, Lupin, how you will repay me when I get my hands on you. I'll recognize you under some cheap disguise, and then, Lupin, you won't brag anymore!

GEORGES: After all, I'm delighted to have the book back so soon. Ganimard, Beautrelet, let's examine the wall and see if we can find the tunnel. It probably won't be of any use, but—

GANIMARD: Agreed, let's have a look at it.

(They examine the wall, as Velmont contemplates the showcase.)

VELMONT (aside): Oh—the mystery of the Hollow Needle.

ELENA (entering with Laura): Here she is, Georges.

GEORGES (caressingly): Ah, Laura, sweeter every day.

LAURA (smiling): Thank you, Georges. I'm glad to see you.

VELMONT (aside, vexed): That's her. She's here.

GEORGES (presenting): Abbé Gelis—

LAURA: I remember –

ABBÉ (saluting): I am delighted to see you again.

GEORGES: My friend, Horace Velmont whom, I am sure, will be an excellent friend to you.

LAURA: My dear— (turning) Him! Could it be him?

VELMONT (bowing): Mademoiselle—

ELENA (noticing Laura's upset): You're pale?

GEORGES: Do you know Laura? Do you know Horace?

VELMONT (who has made his way to the door): I believe so; this young lady ought to remember—

LAURA (as if thinking): Here. Arsène Lupin, here!

(All turn to Lupin questioningly)

LUPIN (arrogantly): Well, yes! I am Arsène Lupin. Bye-bye! Till later! Toodaloo!

(He goes out and closes the door.)

GANIMARD (stupefied): Him! Curses!

(He rushes to the door with Beautrelet, but it is locked.)

CURTAIN

ACT II

Same as Act I.

GEORGES (to his wife): Now that things have calmed down we can have lunch.

ELENA (morose): What if he comes back?

GEORGES (smiling): Who? Arsène Lupin? Don't worry about that, Elena.

ELENA: He said, "Till later."

GEORGES: Bravura! Really, our chateau is surrounded by a cordon of policemen that Mr. Ganimard has favored us with. They've been given the strictest orders. No need to worry, Elena.

ELENA: There's no question I am not at ease. If only Sherlock Holmes were here at least!

LAURA (putting down the book she has been reading): And even if he were! They told us he'd be here at eleven; Sherlock Holmes would be here in an hour. This time, Lupin is not going to dare anything. He looked foolish rushing out. Now Beautrelet and Ganimard have left here to track him down. All the police are in movement and, in a few hours, the famous thief will be captured—be it secretly or with a lot of uproar.

GEORGES: Certainly! By now Lupin is far from here or in hiding, if he's not already in the hands of Ganimard and Beautrelet. It was fortunate that you recognized him.

ELENA: I should say so!

GEORGES: But for that, it would be difficult, except he would have attempted something before the arrival of Holmes. But this time, he lost the hand at cards.

LAURA: Arsène Lupin! Who would have told me that a year after meeting him at the Spa, I would have chanced to meet him in this house. During former days spent with this man, he treated me with the most exquisite proof of gentlemanliness, the most delicate attentions, the most gallant of compliments. You said that I take a bit of interest. True, all gangsters succeed in the same way—by becoming the trusted friend of an illustrious young man—so affable, so good.

ELENA: Just like here. As we presented him to our cousin Stephen—to attract the sympathy of all.

GEORGES: And we cared about him, admired him. We must recognize that, all things considered, Lupin is a man. How sad that he's engaged in such an ignoble profession.

ELENA (indignant): So villainous, you ought to say.

LAURA (with trouble): It's true! How sad!

GEORGES: If Lupin were given to practice good, he would no doubt—But what do I know? Practice evil, and you don't know where it will end. We took him in. He's an artist—a great artist of robbery.

LAURA (with noticeable unease): That I confess!

ELENA (harshly): The Devil take your admiration. For my part, I have no desire to see him again.

GEORGES: You won't see him, Elena. I'm sure that this time Justice will catch up with this disgraced man.

A SERVANT (holding a bunch of letters that he presents to Georges): Sir!

GEORGES (reading): Ganimard, Beautrelet—What's going on? What do they say? Have you gone out to find what's going on?

SERVANT: A thousand pardons, sir, but we have been ordered by the police not to go anywhere. They are watching everywhere.

GEORGES (irritably): Imbecile! Are you already detained by the police?

SERVANT (humbly): Sir?

GEORGES (irascibly): You may leave.

(The servant leaves.)

LAURA (to Elena): There—You see how calm we can be. Now that the Police have—

ELENA: It was the right thing to do.

GEORGES (roughly): No, Elena, it wasn't.

LAURA: Calm down, Georges. The servants won't do anything without orders. And it's better to be a bit excessive in this, rather than miss something.

ELENA: Exactly. They—

GEORGES: Are very torpid.

(Ganimard enters with Beautrelet.)

GANIMARD (bowing): We're back, Monsieur de Thibermesnil.

BEAUTRELET (ditto): Good evening.

GEORGES: I'm sorry. Much has happened, gentlemen. Pardon me, but the servants are very lazy—the ones you detained without—

GANIMARD: I'll take responsibility for this.

ELENA (to Georges): You see.

BEAUTRELET

When we've closed the passage to ourselves—it would be much better to close it to someone else.

GANIMARD: Don't speak of it any more.

LAURA (timidly): But what has detained you? And what about Lupin?

BEAUTRELET (mysteriously): The other man.

GEORGES (avidly): Has he been caught?

GANIMARD (with a comical shake of his head): No.

ELENA (frightened): Has he escaped?

BEAUTRELET: Almost.

LAURA (with foreboding): Ah!

GANIMARD (solemnly): If you like, you can mourn for him.

GEORGES (disgusted): Dead!

LAURA (anguished): Dead!

BEAUTRELET (lugubriously): Yes, there's no more to do.

ELENA (with tears): So much for the life of a man!

GANIMARD: No doubt, a tear—certainly. Lupin was a man, who, all things considered, seemed sympathetic to me. I would have preferred to take him alive, but he no longer is. (emphatically) When we left here to track him down, I was in time to see him jump the garden wall. Following him, Beautrelet jumped the wall, too, and closed the exit to the grotto. Lupin looked around for the agents I had posted in the surroundings, and who were on alert, after hearing my alarm whistle. The way things stood, Lupin couldn't escape any other way except from the rock—precisely. That suited me. Then Lupin attempted forcefully to get back to the chateau, and was in a hurry either to climb up the rock or get to the base of it. In other times, the rock served as a natural defense of the chateau. But I had also posted men there, who approached him. I thought Lupin, would at last yield to my wishes. He tried to get to the base of the rock, but Beautrelet and I got there first; he saw us and continued to climb. For a moment we lost sight of him. The bandit hid in an outcropping. Beautrelet and I discovered him, and, holding our breath, trying not to be seen, we surrounded him. Lupin then squirmed into the place where my agents were concealed—all but one of them rushed out but Lupin leaped out of the way. Under his feet was the abyss, the river. Beautrelet and I circled around cautiously; we understood Lupin was going to be pressed, and in that case—there was a moment of supreme anxiety. Then he leapt into the void, seeking in the waters of the river below a probable salvation, because he swam admirably. Rapidly grasping his intention, a shot escaped my revolver. Lupin let out a sorrowful scream, clutched at space, and, like a wounded bird, fell.

BEAUTRELET: That's the way it was.

LAURA: How disgraceful.

GEORGES: And his body?

GANIMARD: We got down from the rock—not without difficulty, and ran to the river bank; his body wasn't floating. We intended to drag the river from this side, but as the current was strong, we were unable to do so. Tomorrow, no question, the waters will yield the cadaver of the famous thief, Arsène Lupin.

ELENA (with compassion): What a sad end!

BEAUTRELET: Certainly, Madam. In the moment that Ganimard shot I prayed Heaven for the bullet to miss.

LAURA (with pity and aside): And Heaven was deaf—as it is on so many occasions.

GEORGES: You may believe, Ganimard, that I am affected by his story, and lament its sad ending. To shed blood for any cause—even the blood of a thief—

GANIMARDL I recognize that the game ended well. In the end, when Sherlock Holmes gets here, there will be nothing for him to do.

ELENA: And how slow he is.

BEAUTRELET: If any of Lupin's gang are still lurking around, we will keep an eye out for them.

GANIMARD: I suspect we won't see any.

GEORGES: In the end, Ganimard, let's stop this lugubrious conversation and go eat. I hope you'll accept the honors of our table, less as a gift than as an offering from the heart.

LAURA (aside): Ah! How little the life of a man is worth.

GANIMARD (getting up): I warn you that I don't have a great appetite. Things like this actually make me ill.

BEAUTRELET: Me, too, Monsieur Ganimard.

ELENA: Then we won't wait any longer. To eat, gentlemen, and then you will have a place to lie down. (seeing that Laura is furtively wiping away a tear) But, you're crying Laura.

LAURA (attempting to smile): No, no—not crying. How stupid!

GEORGES: Truly, that would be sympathetic. For the last time, shall we go?

LAURA (accepting Georges' arm): Let's go.

(Beautrelet takes Elena's arm and the four start to leave.)

ELENA: Monsieur Ganimard, would you like to put out the lights?

GANIMARD: Gladly, Madame.

ELENA (thoughtfully): But, sir, how the Devil did you shoot so straight? It must have hit him straight in the heart.

(Ganimard puts out the light and follows the others.

(For a moment the stage is lit only by moonlight. After a pause the Letter "H" in Thibermesnil turns and then the "R" slides forward. The bookcase, making a rusty squeaking noise, opens at the "L" in Thibermesnil. At first, no one appears, then Lupin enters silently from the secret door.)

LUPIN: I thought this cursed mechanism would give me away. How noisy! It would be better to grease it; it cannot be avoided. For sure, it hasn't been used in a hundred years— (noticing that the door of the tunnel covers the whole room) Admirable. No one would expect to enter like this. How foresighted were our ancestors of the Middle Ages. And how good were those artisans to suspect that their marvelous work would still be used today, 700 years later, by a well-educated thief! (laughing) Ah, Ganimard, how red-faced you are going to be when you discover my deed. Take good care to read my card. (going to the tunnel entrance, calling) Jeannot! Gomel! Come, quick!

(Jeannot and Gomel enter carrying sacks.)

LUPIN: Look sharp, guys. Carefully detach these pictures, these tapestries. You, Gomel, go to the entrance to the tunnel to inform the other companions. You, Jeannot, detach this tapestry but noiselessly. Let's not waste time.

(As he speaks, his men detach pictures and take various objects.)

LUPIN: Work silently. Take this... Not that one, the other one... Let's go. Hurry, Gomel. This statue, these weapons. Stop—take another sack, Jeannot.

(They rapidly throw small objects into their sacks.)

LUPIN: Take great care of these objects, my friends. (threateningly) That's the way to break something.

GOMEL (humiliated): I'll be careful, sir.

JEANNOT: Anything else to do?

LUPIN: I don't know. Get the others to put all this in the truck, and take it away. You wait at the entrance to the tunnel.

JEANNOT: Fine, sir.

LUPIN: You can withdraw and listen alertly.

GOMEL: We will.

(Gomel follows Jeannot into the tunnel. Lupin starts to go then stops.)

LUPIN: Arsène Lupin—everything is working as you wish. Let's see if the Mystery of the Hollow Needle responds in equal fashion to my wishes. If Abbé Gelis is well informed, in this book I will find a parchment with the mysterious inscription.

(taking the book carefully)

LUPIN: Nothing! Not a sign! Not a clue! After all, there's nothing hidden in it. No, no—I've got it. (very pleased) Yes, yes—Here it is—between the cover and the velvet. This is it, yes. (removing a parchment from the book) This is it! Thanks to me, Arsène Lupin, the secret lair of the Kings of France is no longer a mystery. Oh, it's good that we have Abbés who dedicate themselves to researching historical matters for the benefit of us thieves. (Again he looks at the parchment) Fine, this is a riddle will be deciphered with more time. Let's now leave a note for this stupid Ganimard. By writing on this book, I feel as if I'm committing a sacrilege—but, Bah! (writing) "In everlasting memory, from Arsène Lupin to his dearest friend, Georges de Thibermesnil." It's possible he won't like this very much, but— (firmly) But wouldn't I love to hear the exclamations of the king of detectives, Mr. Sherlock Holmes, when he arrives and sees this? And the curses of Ganimard. Ah, barbarian! He almost got me last night—by the Grace of God, if it hadn't been for my ability to swim—I don't like being under water, I don't feel safe. Bah! It was but an unforeseen night bath! If one must have one, at least one should enjoy it!

(Going to the library intending to open it when Laura enters.)

LAURA (supporting herself if the doorway): Ah!

LUPIN (timid as a schoolboy): Laura!

LAURA (weakly): You! You!

(She almost faints.)

LUPIN (supporting Laura): Don't faint, Laura. I understand that my presence here—

LAURA (trying to get up): My God!

LUPIN: You thought I was dead, right? That's what that beastly Ganimard and that ragamuffin Beautrelet said— they believe it, but luckily I am still alive. See, I am here.

LAURA (bitterly): And why did you return?

LUPIN (understanding the reproach): Oh, it's true, it's true. Around you, around you, who you I love with all my being since I met you at the Spa, I am—please, Laura. Look at me. For you, for the love of you, I am capable of all, of all. As much good as evil!

LAURA: Go away!

LUPIN (supplicating): Laura, if you scorn me as a thief—from now on, I'll be good, honorable.

LAURA: Honorable!

(laughing morosely she starts to leave.)

LUPIN: Laura, if only you knew the enormous pain this irony causes me! If you find me odious as a thief— (calling) Jeannot! Gomel!

JEANNIOT: Sir ?

GOMEL (listening at the door): Listen! People are coming.

LUPIN: The Devil! People are coming. (exaltedly) Escape! Jeannot, this woman—take her!

(Jeannot grabs Laura by her belt and drags her into the tunnel.)

LUPIN: Robbed! We shall see how they think now.

(Lupin leaves with his gang and closes the secret door behind him. The letters in the relief move. Then, silence. Soon Georges enters with Sherlock Holmes followed by Ganimard and Beautrelet. The room is still dark.)

GEORGES: Yes, Mr. Holmes, now you will see!

(turning on the lights and seeing everything has been stolen)

GORGES: Good Heavens!

GANIMARD: Robbed!

BEAUTRELET: Robbed!

HOLMES (somberly): It seems I arrived here too late.

GEORGES: But this is inexplicable!

HOLMES (authoritatively): Gentlemen—don't touch anything.

(He examines the room meticulously.)

GEORGES: Right, Mr. Holmes—please tell me who got in here, and who made off with all these things?

HOLMES (drily): He did.

GEORGES: But—who is he?

HOLMES: Arsène Lupin.

GANIMARD: Then he's alive?

BEAUTRELET: According to him.

GEORGES (furious, to Ganimard): But didn't you say you killed him?

HOLMES (imperturbably): Calm down, Monsieur de Thibermesnil. I don't know this thief personally, but I know this game is dangerous. Inspector Ganimard put away his revolver when Lupin jumped, and saw him flail in space, heard him scream, and saw him fall like an inert being into the water. He thought he had been hit by his bullet—dead. This young man, too.

BEAUTRELET: I believed it—certainly.

HOLMES: As did I, who wasn't there. It was precisely at that moment you should have been more vigilant.

GANIMARD (excusing himself): But, Mr. Holmes—if I had hit him good, and—

HOLMES (smiling): Yes, but you missed.

BEAUTRELET: And we were so sure.

GEORGES (returning with the devotional that Lupin left on the table): And this book. Closed.

BEAUTRELET: This is interesting.

HOLMES (after examining the book): What document was kept in this book?

GEORGES: There wasn't any, Mr. Holmes.

HOLMES: One was kept here.

GEORGES: No, sir—I'm sure of that.

HOLMES (insisting): A very small document—like a page from a notebook.

GEORGES: Again I say—no.

HOLMES (laughing): And I tell you there was. This document was kept here for many years. It was made of heavy paper or parchment Yes, sir, this parchment was hidden between the cover and the velvet. Yes, it was a parchment

GEORGES (admiringly): I think you are right. Something has been torn out. No one knew this book hid anything.

BEAUTRELET (aside to Ganimard): What a man he is, Ganimard!

GANIMARD (aside to Beautrelet): He's a colossus. (to Holmes) What I cannot figure out, Mr. Holmes, is how Lupin, by himself, was able, in the short time that he had in here, to carry away so much and with no noise.

GEORGES: And where to?

HOLMES (smiling): Lupin didn't come alone—he brought two men.

GANIMARD (marveling): Two more men. But how do you know?

HOLMES: You didn't look, you didn't examine. I did. The footprints of these men left tracks on the carpet. (to Beautrelet) Observe, young man.

BEAUTRELET (after looking at the doorway): Indeed. One of them wore wide shoes with studs, and the other—

GEORGES (interrupting him): Fine, but, which way did they enter, and how did they carry off so many jewels?

HOLMES (smiling): Inspector Ganimard?

GANIMARD (who's watched Beautrelet examine the room): I was looking for clues, but—a

HOLMES: You didn't find any?

GANIMARD (disconcerted): No, sir.

HOLMES: Very well—they came this way.

(He goes to the library; the others watch, stupefied)

GEORGES: But this is a book case.

HOLMES: And a door.

BEAUTRELET: That opens—

GEORGES: Yes. How does it open?

HOLMES: You tell me.

GEORGES (stupefied): Me?

GANIMARD: But how did he know—?

HOLMES: He knew because Monsieur de Thibermesnil told him.

GEORGES: Me? You're accusing me?

HOLMES: Yes. Unintentionally, of course. Try to remember.

GEORGES: All we did was—we talked of a tunnel—a secret passage—of the legends surrounding it.

HOLMES: Legends, you say? What are they?

GEORGES: well, first: Thibermesnil-2-6-12.

HOLMES (pensively): Yes, that's one of them

GEORGES: Is it?

GANIMARD: How?

HOLMES: Please, the other one.

GEORGES: *The axe swings in the trembling air, but the ell opens and one journeys towards God.*

GANIMARD: Then we went to dinner.

HOLMES (ironic): Despite so much.

(solemnly matching his actions to his words.)

HOLMES: Monsieur de Thibermesnil—if you want to enter the tunnel, all you have to do is to turn the letter H. (smiling and turning it) *La hache*—the axe—corresponds to the French letter *H* and it does swing. Then *l'air* stands for the letter *R*, which "trembles" when you shake it... (he does) *l'aile* is the letter *L*, which opens and complete the release of the secret mechanism. (The bookcase splits and the secret passage opens.)

GEORGES: What an imbecile I was.

BEAUTRELET: Marvelous.

GANIMARD (entering the tunnel): I'm going to look for Lupin.

HOLMES: Do you have a chapel around here—or a cemetery?

GEORGES: Yes, the chapel and the cemetery of the chateau. Three hundred meters from here.

HOLMES (running to the door): Then it's in this chapel that the tunnel is going to exit. This inscription says so: "*and one journey towards God.*"

ELENA (entering): Laura! Laura! She's gone! But who is this?

HOLMES: Don't worry, Madame. I will recover the stolen goods.

ELENA: My God! My God!

HOLMES: You were asking after Laura. Who is she?

GEORGES: A relative of mine that came today.

HOLMES (thinking aloud): And left with him.

ELENA (shocked): Eh? What are you saying?

HOLMES: Or that he carried her off. It's the same thing.

GEORGES (stunned): But—what do you mean?

HOLMES: It's strange that she came here. Who did this young lady come for?

ELENA: She came here for the novel she was reading. How disgraceful.

HOLMES: Therefore— (thinking aloud) She surprised the thief, probably fainted and was— (solemnly) Miss Laura has been kidnapped.

GEORGES (shocked): By him?

(Holmes nods)

GEORGES: In that case—

(He rushes to the library.)

BEAUTRELET: To save her. Let's go.

HOLMES (imperiously): Calm yourselves, gentlemen. To enter here is to expose oneself to death. For the bandits are in there.

GEORGES:

Who cares? We will go and—

HOLMES: It would be stupid to fight mere thugs unprepared. Monsieur de Thibermesnil, let an automobile be prepared. We are needed at another site.

GEORGES: Yes, Mr. Holmes. Now we'll go all the same.

(leaving with Beautrelet)

ELENA (anguished): And you say you are going to save her?

HOLMES: I trust so. Ah, Arsène Lupin—Sherlock Holmes is on your heels. We shall see.

CURTAIN

ACT III

A crystal gallery. Moonlight illuminates the gallery revealing a leafy park. An electric light hangs from the ceiling. Two doors on one side. There are three doors that are closed.

LUPIN (flowers in hand): For the last time, Laura.

LAURA: I told you—never.

LUPIN: Laura—

LAURA: You are infamous, Lupin: depraved—but never so much as now.

LUPI N(throwing the flowers at Laura's feet.): Please, Laura, don't be crazy, to brave the lion is dangerous. The chivalry of men has limits.

LAURA (ironic): You, chivalrous?

LUPIN: Until today, Laura, I've shown it. My love has been able to control itself; tomorrow—who knows? Get it in your head that my passion could get out of control, and then—when a river overruns its banks, it destroys what it meets in its path. You have one day more. I've been respectful and gallant, and nice, very nice. When tomorrow comes, don't obligate me by your disdain to forget that consideration is owed to a young woman. Because I love you, because I am madly in love with you, and because I don't want to obtain anything violently. Be nice. Think that, in my condition, it would be nice of you to return my love and to tell me so. I don't want you to fear what I am.

LAURA: Why haven't you set me free already?

LUPIN: Because that would mean losing you.

LAURA (ironic): And keeping me here?

LUPIN: You will listen to me.

206

LAURA: I hear you.

LUPIN: And you will love me.

LAURA: That, never!

(She goes into her room and closes the door.)

LUPIN (discouraged): Decidedly, I'm not getting any-where. To her, I'm no more than a thief, degraded, dis-honored. Nothing's working. And all things considered she must belong to me. (pause) She will be what I, Arsène Lupin, wants her to be. I've shown myself lov-ing, submissive, a lover. And not a cruel man! I begged, I wept—and nothing. She threatens me and belittles me.

(pause) And, no question, it's necessary that Laura be my woman. No violence, no rough stuff, Lupin. Let's practice the other idea. Yes, there's no other remedy. A bit of strength—but... (looking at his watch) Now's the time. I don't have time to seek others.

(opening the door)

LUPIN: Ganimard, would you be so good as to come in?

GANIMARD (in cuffs): What do you want with me, bandit?

LUPIN (smiling): Ganimard, I don't think that's a good tone to take with a friend. Are you in a bad mood?

GANIMARD (sharply): And what's that to you?

LUPIN (always laughing) You are going to see what it is to me. I don't want, when you leave here, to send you back to your wife in a debilitated condition. Come, Ganimard, I offer you something else. Do you need something else? You know that you don't have much to lose. I desire to help you.

GANIMARD (irritated): Bandit!

LUPIN (phlegmatically): Again? You've always had this defect. Never able to control your nerves. It's the only quality that you lack. If you weren't in such a hurry you would be the best of cops—almost the equal of Sherlock Holmes.

GANIMARD (furious): Go to hell! You are joking!

LUPIN: Calm down, Ganimard. You don't appreciate the value of patience at times. Let's have a look. What do you gain by infuriating yourself with despair? Uniquely bored, bad things happen. And you cannot complain of the housing—nice bed, nice table, servants that serve you without putting you to the trouble of calling them. You are treated like a king. Don't be displeased, Ganimard: ingratitude is the worst of sins.

GANIMARD (brutally): It's for this that you brought me in here? The more you make me value my freedom. (roaring) Oh, once I'm free, I will get you!

LUPIN (laughing): I like that, Ganimard. That is well reasoned. A cop is always a cop. Now, you are in my power and ought to be resigned, but once out of here—if you ever do get out—you will try to avenge yourself. There, you see how frank I am. If someday, I decided to set you free—I don't know when or why—but you would be perfectly within your rights to seize me, if you are capable of it—or fire a shot at me. Despite all that—with a thief like me—shouldn't you consider what you are doing?

GANIMARD (still furious): Let me rot here! You think that I'm going to rot here! Meanwhile, Sherlock Holmes is pursuing you, and I retain the hope he will free me from you.

LUPIN (laughing uproariously): Sherlock Holmes!

GANIMARD: Sherlock Holmes, yes. He will save me. And if not, Beautrelet will. And if not Beautrelet, I will escape myself.

LUPIN (still laughing): Ganimard, Holmes is hoping you will liberate him.

GANIMARD: Huh? What?

LUPIN: I mean that Holmes—don't make such a face, Ganimard! That Holmes, like you, is my prisoner.

GANIMARD (furious and incredulous): You lie!

LUPIN: This morning—this good British friend of yours was a bit worried, you know, Ganimard. And as for me, why, naturally, I profited from it. You shall hear the outcome. It's very diverting. You shall see. You know that, as soon as Sherlock Holmes got here, he did a lot of work to destroy me. In a week, he'd done me more harm than you and Beautrelet, and you were on my trail for a long while. Fine—then Sherlock discovered that Clotilde was my accomplice, and thought—it was a fine thought—to seize her, and make her sing. Thinking about her this morning, he rented an automobile and went up to capture Clotilde, and with her, satisfied by his work, climbed back into the automobile. He gave signs to the driver, and what a laugh, Ganimard, the car left Paris like an arrow, and brought him here. The chauffeur steering his car was me.

GANIMARD: You lie, Lupin, you lie! No! Once Holmes suspected the change in direction of the automobile, once he observed the direction it was taking—

LUPIN (still laughing): You guessed it Ganimard, but he suspected too late, and the vehicle was running at maximum speed.

GANIMARD: You were risking a shot.

LUPIN: You are very stupid, beloved Ganimard. If Holmes had a revolver, he would have—

GANIMARD: He never goes anywhere without it.

LUPIN: But, suppose it had been taken from him?

GANIMARD: By whom?

LUPIN: By Clotilde, his prisoner. You really don't know how valuable Clotilde is. Fine—perhaps Sherlock

Holmes would have tried to fire from the carriage, if he had his revolver. Still there was a smash up, but as other friends of mine came out of the other car—let's drop the subject here and—

GANIMARD: My word, Lupin—very well contrived. But I don't believe you. Holmes is not in your power.

LUPIN: Now you shall see him, immediately, as I desire to move him from his room. He'll be brought here, next to you. You'll be less bored, you can pass the time chatting with each other. (calling at the door) Gomel, bring the other prisoner. Be careful with him, he's very clever.

GANIMARD (stupefied) Why—is it possible?

LUPIN: Now you shall see.

GANIMARD: And Beautrelet, too?

LUPIN: No, not yet. But I'll catch him in a few days. He knows too much. This kid is starting to annoy me.

(Holmes in handcuffs, enters, smiling, as if untroubled by being a prisoner.)

GANIMARD (at the sight of him): So it is true, Mr. Holmes.

HOLMES: Hello, Inspector.

LUPIN (deferentially): Pardon, esteemed Sherlock Holmes, if I've kept you lodged for some hours in circumstances less than a man like you deserves. But, there it is, repairing my fault. From now on you can dispose of these quarters and of this gallery if you think it suitable.

HOLMES (seriously): It's all the same to me.

LUPIN: Why is it that this morning we can't seem to understand each other? (calling) Gomel, Jeannot. Don't be lazy. Don't you see Mr. Holmes is hurting? Loosen his handcuffs.

HOLMES: It doesn't matter.

LUPIN: Now, it's better. I've always admired you, and it pains me greatly to see myself obliged to keep you in my power for a few days—but it's necessary, so that I can finish some pending business.

GANIMARD (exalted): But, see here, Lupin—are you boasting, by coming here to tell us how many robberies you've got going?

LUPIN: Ganimard, you are incorrigible. I take a moment to tell you the beauties of calm and you won't have any of it, you don't want to listen. Learn from Mr. Sherlock Holmes. Don't you see? Smiling imperturbably.

GANIMARD: May the Devil take you, cursed Lupin.

HOLMES: I warn you, Lupin, that if you have more to tell me, be quick about it, I am going to sleep.

LUPIN: I'll be short, Mr. Holmes. As I suspect, you were thinking of better things. I hope to rectify the opinion of this morning. I know you, sir. If you will give me your word of honor not to bother about me for the next week, you are free as of this moment, or if not, tomorrow at dawn, you will be aboard a steamer I own and you will be traveling for a while.

HOLMES (calmly): Ah, don't persist, Lupin. I will do what I can to frustrate your plans.

GANIMARD (with enthusiasm): Ah, very well said.

LUPIN: You are very stubborn, Mr. Holmes, but you see, I am offering you an alternative situation. Give me your word of honor not to try to escape from this house, from this park, just for a week, and you won't be troubled by anything in the future.

HOLMES (imperturbably): I give you my word of honor to be thinking every minute how to escape from here. If I succeed, good; if I don't succeed, I'll be patient.

GANIMARD (enthusiastically): Put that in your pipe and smoke it!

LUPIN: I'm offering you your freedom, Mr. Holmes.

HOLMES: I don't want it from your hands, Mr. Lupin.

LUPIN: Is that your last word?

HOLMES (firmly): It is!

LUPIN: In that case, Mr. Holmes, forgive me for employing some violence; it's your own fault. (To Jeannot and Gomel) Men, tie his hands . Fasten them carefully. (They do.)

GANIMARD (furious): What a scandal!

LUPIN: Life is a game, Ganimard. Today, I tie up Sherlock Holmes. If he has the opportunity, he will tie me up.

HOLMES: That time will come.

LUPIN: For the moment, it seems unlikely, Mr. Holmes.

HOLMES: The next time, it will be easy, Mr. Lupin.

LUPIN: We agree about that. Finally, I shall withdraw. I'll be back tomorrow around this time—or a bit later. It depends on my work. Tomorrow, I'll attempt to reason with you again, to settle this business, and convince you to accept my proposals.

HOLMES: Don't trouble yourself about that!

LUPIN: Ta-ta, Mr. Holmes, Ta-ta, Ganimard. A warning—in order to avoid any unpleasantries. I've posted armed sentinels at the exits and also at the foot of the balcony which is across from this gallery. So, that you don't end by breaking your neck. The password of my sentinels is done in an act—and my people are better shots than you, Ganimard.

GANIMARD (furious): This is irritating

HOLMES: Calm down, Inspector, calm down.

LUPIN: Come on, let's go, fellows. Some of you stay near the door in case these gentlemen need something. And you know they deserve our utmost consideration— they are our guests.

(Gomel, Jeannot and Lupin leave. Then Ganimard goes to Holmes to untie him.)

HOLMES (smiling): What are you doing, Mr. Ganimard? Please don't touch me.

GANIMARD (not understanding): But—to leave you like this? Lupin was stupid. He didn't untie you, but I can.

HOLMES (impassively): No, Mr. Ganimard, Lupin is not stupid. When he left us here alone together, he had a reason. He is confident we cannot escape.

GANIMARD: Fine—suppose we cannot escape, this rope still bothers you and—

HOLMES: It doesn't bother me. Quiet now.

GANIMARD (still untying Holmes): Why, no, sir, I don't think that a man like you should be roped up.

HOLMES: You are very stubborn. Do what I say.

GANIMARD: Pardon me for once, Mr. Holmes, for trying to untie you.

(At this moment the door opens. Jeannot and Gomel enter pointing revolvers at Ganimard.)

JEANNOT: Bravo, Mr. Ganimard! Is this the way you repay the hospitality we've extended to you?

GANIMARD (furious): The nerve! Did you hear that, Mr. Holmes?

HOLMES: I heard, my friend, I heard—But it's your stubbornness that got you in trouble.

JEANNOT (coming in): Mr. Ganimard, back to your cell. You deserve more punishment for disobeying.

GANIMARD: Eh? Eh? Did you hear that? You are lacking in respect, young man!

JEANNOT: Back to your cell, I said!

HOLMES: Obey, Mr. Ganimard. You asked for it.

(They force Ganimard into his cell and lock the door.)

JEANNOT: Pardon me, sir, but I have to tighten the ropes a bit now that your friend insisted on untying it.

(He tightens the ropes.)

JEANNOT: And now, if you need anything, command us.

HOLMES: Yes, open the door of my room, I want to get some sleep.

(They open his door, and they leave.)

HENRIETTA (calling to see if the door is closed.)
Laura, my dear, open up—it's me.

LAURA (opening and smiling): Henrietta!

HENRIETTA: I'm bringing you some cold meat, as you didn't want anything before at dinner.

LAURA (interrupting her): I don't want any, no, I would be sick.

HENRIETTA: Bah! Have some food, Laura, or you'll wind up sick.

(Gomel and Jeannot emerge from Holmes' room.)

GOMEL: Have a nice night, Miss.

JEANNIOT: Until tomorrow, Miss.

(Laura replies with a constrained gesture.)

HENRIETTA: Let's go, Laura. Where do you want dinner—here or somewhere else? Look, it's less hot here. Would you like me to open some window?

LAURA: What for?

HENRIETTA: Eh! We have a table here—a bit inconvenient, but— (pulling out a bottle of wine) Come on, Laura, this chicken is almost edible without appetite.

LAURA: No, not now, Henrietta. Let me alone. Maybe later.

HENRIETTA: My friend, what are you ill about? Wouldn't it be better to talk it over?

LAURA: No, Henrietta, talk it over. What? Your son should think it over. You ought to make him understand he's being obstinate in keeping me here. A woman's heart is unmoved, unmoved by violence unless there is love.

HENRIETTA: You're right. But as for him—precisely because he loves you, he's keeping you here. No rush as you say. Presently, you are regaled like a princess, your least caprices are obeyed by a legion of servants.

LAURA: I've been deprived of my liberty. Kept shut up here for thirty days without any fault of mine. It's certain, without doing anything, which offends me; without doing anything, he's venturing to see me with disdain. All of you serve me, all of you watch over me to take care of me, and each day that passes, each hour that goes by, nonetheless brings a new martyrdom to my heart.

HENRIETTA: I understand your repugnance, Laura. It's natural you shun my poor Arsène. He loves no one but you. He shows you love, but you don't show any love in return for him. And instead of loving him, you hate him.

LAURA: No, that, no. You see, Henrietta, you who've been so good to me, you who never leave my side except to do something impossible to please me, you who are a woman, you understand very well the sorrows of my soul, the bitterness of my life.—I don't hate Arsène—at least until today, I didn't hate him. My heart doesn't know hate—maybe not tenderness. But I cannot love him. I cannot do it, and I won't do it. (firmly) I don't want to! When I met him at the Spa, under an assumed name, when he was pouring gallant phrases in my ear, and I saw him glad to serve me, I came to sympathize with such a fine gentleman—so likable. For he was a gentleman! But, when a bit later he lied to me, and Mr. Ganimard came to arrest him, whatever sympathy I had was extinguished, destroyed. The gentleman courting me was a thief. What horror! But now, above all, now I am offended, because abusing my situation, he kidnapped me, separated me from my family, keeps me here against my will, against all right. For Arsène, I am no more than an agreeable object that he stole to add to his collection of jewels, of paintings, of—

HENRIETTA (interrupting here with tenderness): No, Laura. For my son, my poor son, lost on the path of life, you are more, much more than you imagine. Ah, if you wanted to you could make my poor son a good man, an honorable man.

LAURA (with pain): Nothing can be made of your son—but what he is.

HENRIETTA: You hesitate, Laura. I'm sure, very sure of what I say; and, if I were not certain that you could regenerate my poor son, I would not have neglected to free the door of this house. Help me to save him—for pity. Help me, Laura. An unhappy mother asks you, weeping, on her knees—at your feet.

LAURA: Poor mother, all goodness and all suffering.

HENRIETTA (coaxing): Will you help me, Laura?

LAURA: I cannot, Henrietta, I cannot. To save him from himself—if he could be saved—I would have to be-smirch myself, and Laura de Saint-Veran cannot be-smirch herself. I cannot lower myself to accept the hand of a thief. To be his prisoner, to spend my whole life here—that I can do. But never will Laura de Saint-Veran be able to listen with complacency to the gallantries of Arsène Lupin! Never!

HENRIETTA: Never!

(She hides her head in her hands, weeping. Laura heads to her dwelling, but a flash of lightning stops her.)

HENRIETTA: Did you see that, Laura? Don't be afraid. I say, little girl, that the lightning are sparks released by the anger of God—that we owe to his goodness. He beats us down into wisdom and makes a saint, and—

(Another flash of lightning illuminates the stage. Thunder.)

LAURA (seeking refuge in Henrietta's arms): What a fright!

HENRIETTA: Frightened—you that are so good.

LAURA: Henrietta, let's get out of here. Let's get going. I'm scared.

HENRIETTA: And where will we go that we won't hear the resounding thunder, that the Heavens send! Where will my Arsène go to escape the lashes of honorable people or the painful voice of justice?

LAURA: Let's go in to my quarters, to bury my face in my pillow, and at least not see the livid light of the lightning.

HENRIETTA: Yes, my friend. (calling) Jeannot, Gomel.

JEANNOT (entering): The lady wishes?

GOMEL: Is the young lady afraid? Oh, don't fear anything.

JEANNOT: We will be here.

LAURA: Thanks, guys. We can talk. Don't worry about me.

(She goes with Henrietta to her dwelling. More rain)

JEANNOT: I haven't eaten yet.

GOMEL: I think the boss is wasting time crying over Miss Laura 'cause she doesn't want him.

JEANNOT: She will. With time.

GOMEL (shaking his head) No, in the end, she'll leave. (looking at the meal Laura wouldn't eat) Doesn't this chicken—?

JEANNOT: Hungry, Gomel?

GOMEL: What about you?

JEANNOT: Not very. But, you know—eat and scrape.

GOMEL: You're always strong, Jeannot, and, after all, life is spent this way.

(swallowing some chicken meat.)

JEANNOT (getting ready to eat): Listen, listen—don't eat so fast, I want some, too.

GOMEL: Then eat. (munching) The truth is that—(stopping chewing) In these situations, truth is a distracting thing. (goes back to chewing)

JEANNOT (masticating): Figuring?

GANIMARD: Jeannot, Jeannot!

GOMEL (without interrupting his eating) I bet that Ganimard has heard the noise of your jaws, and wants to drink something.

(taking the wine bottle and drinking)

GANIMARD (calling): Jeannot—don't you hear me?

JEANNOT (without moving): Coming. (munching slowly)

GANIMARD: Come on, man. Don't you hear me calling you?

JEANNOT (imperturbably): Coming. (munching without any signs of moving)

GOMEL: Don't you want some chicken. You haven't dined.

GANIMARD (furious): Jeannot, you beast! What are you doing?

JEANNOT (with his mouth full): Coming.

GANIMARD (furious): Thus you quench yourself, animal!

GOMEL (drinking): There's a gentleman ill brought up.

JEANNIOT (opening the door to Ganimard's cell): What can I offer you?

GANIMARD: Bring me some water.

JEANNOT: Coming.

HOLMES: Gomel.

JEANNOT: Do you hear, Gomel. Be attentive. You know what the boss will say.

HOLMES: Gomel.

GOMEL (getting up slowly, wiping his face with a napkin): Coming.

(opening Holmes' door)

GOMEL: What do you order?

HOLMES: First that you attend me as soon as you are called, and afterwards—bring me a beer.

GOMEL: Fine, sir. All of us are a bit thirsty.

(going to get a beer)

GANIMARD: Jeannot.

GOMEL (returning with a beer): Ganimard's calling you.

JEANNOT: I heard him. He's most annoying. (to Ganimard) What do you want with me?

GANIMARD: That you don't answer me ill. Open the door for me.

JEANNOT: Where are you going?

GANIMARD: Nowhere. I want to drink in the breeze.

HOLMES: Gomel.

GOMEL: Sir?

HOLMES: I want to come out.

GOMEL(to Jeannot): Did you hear? You go for him. He damned goes in and out all night.

GANIMARD: Eh! Eh. Did you hear that? Foul mouthed.

HOLMES: I only want to smoke.

GOMEL: Well, sir. As for that ,we have cigarettes—cigarillos—

HOLMES (interrupting him): I don't want your tobacco, I have some of my own in this package. American. Want one?

(Gomel reaches into Holmes' coat and fishes out a pack of cigarettes.)

HOLMES: There. Light one for me.

JEANNOT: This ought to be good tobacco.

(puffing)

JEANNOT (smiling): This is delightful.

GANIMARD: Make way for me, man. Lazybones! Daring, but lacking shame.

HOLMES: Calm down, Mr. Ganimard. Don't you see how I am taking it?

GOMEL (taking a cigarette): If you would permit me, sir?

GANIMARD: But how can we live here like this? Can we endure these shameless people?

HOLMES (calmly): Smoke it, Gomel. And when you are finished, light one for me.

GOMEL: Ah, yes, pardon me. I'll light another.

GANIMARD: But have you gone mad? That's the second one you are smoking.

GOMEL: Ah, it's true, forgive me! Now I'll light another.

GANIMARD: And you, Jeannot. What are you doing? Get up!

(Holmes motions for him to shut up.)

GOMEL: He's gone to sleep. Let's finish dinner. (falling asleep) And, me, too—I'm sleepy. What great cigarettes. (He falls asleep.)

HOLMES: Quick, quick, Mr. Ganimard. Now, untie me. Let's go.

(Ganimard unties him.)

HOLMES: Those cigarettes are opiate-filled. Hurry, Mr. Ganimard. (listening) Eh? Listen! I hear noise—coming this way. Quickly, Mr. Ganimard, more quickly!

(Beautrelet enters with Lupin disguised as Luis Valmeras, a young man of thirty.)

BEAUTRELET: Mr. Ganimard.

GANIMARD: That voice. It's Beautrelet.

BEAUTRELET: It's me, Mr. Ganimard! I am with a friend.

HOLMES: We are saved.

(Beautrelet and Lupin force the door open.)

BEAUTRELET: And what about Laura?

(Lupin deliberately heads in the wrong direction.)

GANIMARD: Not that way, not that way. To the right.

BEAUTRELET (finishing untying Holmes and Ganimard): Luis Valmeras is a friend of mine—You know him? Fine fellow. (pointing to Lupin) Without him, I doubt I'd have been able to save you. (seeing Jeannot and Gomel.) And these two?

HOLMES: Asleep. Stupefied by the opium in my cigarettes.

(Laura is led out of her room by Lupin. The others leave.)

LUPIN (changing his voice) Take care of this young lady. There's an old hag in there who must be an accomplice. I'm going for her.

LAURA: No, no—for God's sake. Don't hurt her. She's very good.

HOLMES: Moreover, we will be delayed. It will be difficult for us to leave.

GANIMARD: We are free. I can breathe.

BEAUTRELET: Let's get out of here. Our friends are waiting down there.

LAURA: Free at last.

(She takes Lupin's arm.)

HOLMES: I will avenge myself, Arsène Lupin. I'm going to get you!

CURTAIN

ACT IV

A hexagonal room in the Hollow Needle. On one side, there is a huge triptych. The room is lavishly furnished with art objects of all types, paintings, statues, etc. Two heavy doors are at the back. Lupin, still disguised as Luis Valmeras, is writing checks to his henchmen and associates.

LUPIN: Charlois, you get 30,000 francs. You can cash it tomorrow at the Credit Lyonnais. Nice to have yours. Bremil, 40,000 francs. (laughing) You like it a lot, Garliot—you are only getting 12,000 francs, not a penny more. Ah, here's what you get, David. And yours, Valentin. Nice pickings, 50,000 francs each. Very good, Gomel, Jeannot, you'll get a little fortune. (putting his pen away.) Now, my friends, goodbye. With this money, if you show some industry, some sort of business sense, you can live honorably. We shan't see each other again. I'll open my shop like a gypsy in some foreign country. You can leave now. Ah, go out by the stairway on the right.
(shakes hands with his associates as they file by.)
LUPIN: Goodbye.
(He hugs some; wipes away a furtive tear.)
GOMEL: Sir, I would like to beg a favor.
LUPIN: Speak, Gomel.
GOMEL: So I am not dismissed from your service. Wherever you go, you will need someone to serve you, and I—
LUPIN (moved): Ah, faithful dog! Fine! You shall stay with me.
GOMEL (very happy): Thank you, sir.

LUPIN: Listen, Gomel. I appoint you watchman at my farm in Neuville. You will go there immediately—but before you do, talk to Blechot—I want to install new gates that will snap shut.

GOMEL: That snap shut after the visitor passes through?

LUPIN: Afterwards, yes. You can withdraw.

(Gomel leaves)

LUPIN: It's over with. Over with. Her shame is over. But her love, her tranquility is well worth this sacrifice.

(rings a bell. Jeannot enters.)

LUPIN: The lady?

JEANNOT: Waiting, sir.

LUPIN: Tell her, I'm waiting for her. And you can prepare the table for three persons.

(Jeannot nods and leaves.)

LUPIN: I would never have believed it. Tomorrow, all of Europe will question if Lupin has indeed, painstakingly, gone to Hell. There will be no more inexplicable robberies, no more improbable kidnappings, no more extraordinary deeds. Oh, and many people will be bored in the future. The newspapers will appear without an exciting story, defrauding public curiosity. One day, they will speak of me, of my disappearance in the Hollow Needle—that famous lair that I will definitively abandon, and then—nothing! Sherlock Holmes won't be there to solve difficult problems, nor will I be afraid of returning to meet Ganimard, that brute of Ganimard. As for Beautrelet who is congratulating himself on having penetrated the secret of my hideout— (ironic) He won't understand that I, alone, carelessly brought him here, permitted him to enter here. Oh, the vanity of men!

(meeting Laura)

LAURA: My wife! How complacent you are! Later we will lunch here, and right after—my mother at Neuville awaits us there—impatiently. My mother.

LAURA: How nice that will be. If I didn't love you so much, I wouldn't be able to live here inside this boring rock, that's bathed lovingly by the waters of Le Havre. But—it's so sad. Without being able to see the fields, or being able to hear under the trees that loaned me their shade in my childhood, without being able to walk about the beloved garden, pulling out flowers with my own hands, to put them in my hair, without small things that remind me of my life. I was born to make your life happy by loving you, adoring you like a god. But like the nightingale, by making your life happy, it's also necessary to live in the full sun, without somersaults, without worries, with you—you and me alone. What happiness!

(Jeannot enters sets the table then withdraws.)

LUPIN: Alone? What about my mother?

LAURA: Your mother and I, we are no more than one, confused in my heart into a single immense tenderness. The tenderness of your poor old lady.

(Jeannot returns with three plates and withdraws.)

LUPIN: Thank you, my friend If someday I were to say that happiness was a woman, I would accept your refusing protest with a smile. And no doubt, my Laura, you've convinced me, conquered me, made me believe, made me good. It's the prodigy of love, my wife.

LAURA: What are you thinking? Is something bothering you?

LUPIN: To the contrary, Laura, to the contrary. But yes, I'm the one who's been negligent. You are the best, the most noble, the most holy of all the creatures. And I am there, at your side, complacently, being docile, obedient, timid, trembling with love when you look at me, when you caress me, even when you quarrel with me.

LAURA: I quarrel with you because I adore you, because I tremble that there will come a day when our happiness can be abruptly broken. But no—truly, it can never be broken—nothing can ever finish our marriage

LUPIN: Nothing!

JEANNOT: Whenever you please. (aside) Our two lovebirds seem very happy.

LUPIN (consulting his watch): Twelve o'clock. It's time. You can withdraw, Jeannot—I will call you if I need you.

(Jeannot leaves.)

LAURA: These settings—

LUPIN (laughing): Yes. It's true, I didn't tell you. We've got company.

LAURA: Today? Really, I thought—

LUPIN: That we would be dining alone? No, my friend, we will be accompanied by our old friend Isidore Beautrelet. Yes, it's true, without his concurrence, without his help, Luis Valmeras wouldn't have obtained the heart of Laura de Saint-Veran. Therefore, it's just that today he should be with us for lunch.

LAURA (timidly): Of course. When did you invite him?

LUPIN: I didn't invite him, but I know he will come; he must be coming. I think he will be here shortly. At the entrance door.

LAURA (timidly): Could he have discovered the secret of the Hollow Needle?

LUPIN: No—he hasn't discovered a thing. He was shown the way, he was given all sorts of clues, that gave him the taste to visit the Hollow Needle today, and dine with us. And he, without suspecting a thing, without recognizing my hand, did what he was supposed to do—

He's a good kid. (changing his tone) Laura—meanwhile, I will help give the final hand to our baggage, if he comes before we go.

LAURA (trembling): And Beautrelet is coming alone?

LUPIN (jovial): No, but don't be afraid.

(They leave. The stage remains empty, then Beautrelet enters.)

BEAUTRELET: I don't trust too much in my strength or in my wit. It's prudent not to play with danger. Greetings, King of the Hollow Needle. Greetings! (entering, revolver in hand) No one here. Nothing . Decidedly, you are not in the Needle. Cursed Lupin! There I am forced to climb the stairway. And Ganimard will be impatient downstairs. (seeing the table) Ah, the table is set. Three settings. We need to know with whom we are dealing. (examining the place settings) Monsieur Arsène Lupin, Madame Arsène Lupin— (stunned) Lupin, married! Married! (smiling) And after all, why not? He's a man like all the others. (looking at the third card) Isidore Beautrelet!!

LUPIN (entering, employing the voice and manners of Valmeras): How curious! (He laughs.)

BEAUTRELET (surprised): Eh!

LUPIN (still laughing, holding his arms out wide): My dear Beautrelet!

BEAUTRELET (stupefied): Ah, why it's you, Luis Valmeras? You, Valmeras!

LUPIN: And why not? I am your friend Valmeras, or better yet, Arsène Lupin. (removing his disguise) I am Valmeras, as before I was Horace Velmont. As the other day, I was the shepherd who showed you the way to this place, and before that, the Spanish diplomat that instructed you about a very rare parchment, because it was the key to the mysterious Hollow Needle. Arsène Lupin is always whoever he wants to be. (jovial) And I disguise myself sufficiently well, don't I? I don't give myself away easily from what I see.

BEAUTRELET (confused): But—if you are Lupin—if you are Louis Valmeras—then your wife is—

LUPIN (interrupting him): You guessed it, my friend. (presenting Laura) Madame Arsène Lupin.

BEAUTRELET (stupefied): Laura de Saint-Veran!

LUPIN (correcting him): No, no. The legitimate wife of Arsène Lupin, or if you prefer of Luis Valmeras, your friend and servant. (to Laura) But you see what a frightening face this friend has. Move, Laura, so he can get a better look at you.

LAURA (offering her hand to Beautrelet): Monsieur Beautrelet.

BEAUTRELET (bowing): Madame. I confess I am astonished. All this is quite—astonishing.

LAURA (laughing): On the contrary, Monsieur Beautrelet, very natural.

LUPIN: Don't you understand anything? Yes, it's very simple. Arsène Lupin didn't succeed in obtaining the love of his prisoner Laura de Saint-Veran—but he loved her with determination. And it was imperative that Laura be his. To conquer her, that rascal of a Lupin, conceived of pretending to be Luis Valmeras, the friend of Beautrelet, and helped to rescue Laura, Ganimard and Sherlock Holmes from the clutches of the thief. Do you remember, Isidore? You were grateful, right? Therefore, it happened exactly as it happened. Luis Valmeras, the savior, with Beautrelet, of Laura, the loved one. Valmeras was brought in. Rich, and above all, a gentleman. Laura sympathized with him, and they got married. For sure, Isidore was the witness of this marriage—

exactly six months ago today. Beautrelet, the detective, was godfather of Lupin.

BEAUTRELET (stupefied): Each time, I am more stunned, confounded.

LAURA (interrupting him): Don't think about it, and let's enjoy our meal. But, friend Beautrelet, it's suitable that Laura de Saint Veran is the spouse of Louis Valmeras—or Arsène Lupin—as you please.

BEAUTRELET: To fail to know myself, my own. Who would have thought—

JEANNOT (pulling in a cart loaded with dishes and serving the table): Sir.

LUPIN: That's enough here. Bring us some wine.

BEAUTRELET (talking to himself): But how the Devil could I suspect that Luis Valmeras was Arsène Lupin— my friend Valmeras rescues the woman he loved. How was I to suspect that Lupin was working against Lupin?

LAURA: You don't go against; you go in favor, as you've seen.

BEAUTRELET: Right, right.

LUPIN (after having served Laura, serves Beautrelet): Fine, let's leave it at that. I excuse you, friend. Today, content yourself with cold cuts; we dismissed the cook. No, listen to something else, truly, extraordinary. (speaking slowly) Today, I am definitely abandoning this retreat and my adventurous life. Do you find that strange? Laura has convinced me that honor has inappreciable enchantments. Love causes miracles, Isidore.

BEAUTRELET (serious): Are you joking?

LAURA: What he's telling you is the complete truth. As of today, Arsène Lupin has died morally. Luis Valmeras, the honored and honest Valmeras that you know, will be the one who remains and goes forward wherever he wants.

LUPIN: Let's drink to that.

(They all drink and clink glasses.)

LUPIN: Because, for me to leave this rock that the kings of France used to guard their treasures and sheltered their greatness, is no small thing. When I first got here, it was in very poor condition, and I spent a lot of money repairing it, and I introduced notable improvements. Thus, in just one year that I've occupied this hollow rock, I've brought together here more wealth in pictures, in tapestries, in historic jewels than are in all the museums of Europe. I was speaking seriously. If we have time, I will show you around all these treasures—if not, someday you will see them.

BEAUTRELET: And how do you think you got such great riches?

LAURA: Something very beautiful, Beautrelet, something France will pardon Arsène Lupin for his deeds—something that France will greatly pardon.

LUPIN: Although you, the detectives and the police, judge me to be a disgrace to my fatherland, France will, thanks to me, have the greatest museum in the world. All these pictures, all these tapestries, these jewels, these porcelains that I've brought together here with skill and money, will be bequeathed to my country, Beautrelet. If I stole, if I obtained thousands and thousands of precious historical things from the private galleries and from many nations, it was to be able to say today to my country, "Take these riches, all the world will envy you the luck of possessing it." If I did evil—

(hammering on the downstairs door)

LAURA: Arsène! Do you hear? I am afraid.

LUPIN (calmly): Don't you worry, Laura. (to Jeannot) Accompany the Lady, Jeannot. (to Laura) Go calmly, my dear. Till later.

BEAUTRELET: Madame, we will see each other later.

LAURA: Goodbye, Monsieur Beautrelet. Whenever you like.

LUPIN (jovially): I don't know—you won't see her before you leave here. (to Jeannot) Accompany her and don't leave her for a moment. If something else happens, inform me.

JEANNOT: Understood, sir.

(Leaves with Laura.)

LUPIN: That Ganimard is very impatient. What's keeping them below? Lingering to demolish the doors, I suppose? It's Ganimard's style.

BEAUTRELET: It is indeed.

LUPIN: Can I know how many agents are with him?

BEAUTRELET: Fifty.

LUPIN (laughing): How absurd. Fifty men to take Lupin. And exactly when Lupin was disposed to change his life.

BEAUTRELET (incredulous): But—is it really true what you were telling me?

LUPIN (gravely): Isidore, Arsène Lupin steals, but he never lies. It surprises you that I am abandoning this life, this place? Don't imagine that it didn't cost me a lot to reach this decision. When Laura proposed it to me for the first time, I laughed. Today—today, I desire it just as much as she does, more than she, if that were possible. Laura's love has regenerated me.

(The hammering is getting louder, closer.)

BEAUTRELET: I understand. No question, it would have been better for you to have taken this decision prior to today. Knowing that we had discovered the place, now one might believe you were afraid.

LUPIN (laughing): Afraid? Afraid? Of whom? Of you that I brought here, because I myself have shown you the way to this concealed rock, in my various disguises? But did you conceive you had discovered Lupin and the Hollow Needle? Is that it?

BEAUTRELET: No, it's not just I. It's Ganimard—and Sherlock Homes. Human Justice.

LUPIN (ironic): Ganimard—that brute from whose hands I've escaped a thousand times after surrendering myself to him, so as to attach myself to Holmes whom I tricked when I wanted to, that I deceived like you, that I kept prisoner, and who now is looking for me in the streets of Paris? To Justice in whose prisons I enter to organize my enterprises, and from whose prisons I escape when I want to? Recall al the episodes of my life. Recall if it is true what I'm telling you—recall!

BEAUTRELET (interrupting him): All the same.

LUPIN (more seriously): No, Isidore, Arsène Lupin is not afraid when fifty men come against him. Arsène Lupin does not know fear.

(The noise gets louder. Ganimard has broken through the doors downstairs and is now pounding on the doors to this room.)

GANIMARD: Courage, men, keep going, ah! Ah, bandit, wait till I get you!

LUPIN (laughing obstreperously): Bravo, Ganimard. You're coming in ill humor.

GANIMARD: More effort, men!

POLICEMEN: These doors are not giving way. They are very strong.

LUPIN: I think, Beautrelet, that Ganimard doesn't want us to talk to each other.

BEAUTRELET: That's your fault. Open the door.

LUPIN: No, Beautrelet. They've damaged the one down stairs. Let them damage these.

GANIMARD: Make an effort here. They will give way Ah, bandit of a Lupin, what harm have you done to Beautrelet?

LUPIN: Yes, he really is an imbecile. (yelling at the door) Hey, Ganimard! (The pounding stops.) When have I ever harmed friends?

GANIMARD (furious): Open, Lupin!

LUPIN (calmly): No, dear old chum, you open. But with less noise, because Beautrelet and I are talking about some interesting matters, and we're having trouble hearing each other.

GANIMARD: Men, beat down this door!

(The hammering begins again with renewed energy.)

LUPIN: Decidedly, this brute of a Ganimard is obstinate in preventing me from saying to you what I need to.

(An axe blow penetrates the door, and soon Ganimard's arm with a revolver can be seen poking through the door.)

GANIMARD: Surrender, Lupin!

BEAUTRELET: Arsène Lupin, I take you prisoner in the name of the law.

LUPIN (laughing): You, too, Isidore? (serenely) Intimate to Arsène Lupin that he should surrender. Goodbye, Beautrelet, Goodbye, Ganimard.

(Beautrelet blocks Lupin's escape in one direction. Lupin thinks he can duck behind the triptych, but Ganimard fires his gun and aims at the painting. Lupin leaps out of the line of fire.)

LUPIN: Don't be barbaric, Ganimard. Don't you see you have damaged a great work of art? And above all, aim better. It's twice you've missed the target.

(Beautrelet is petrified by Lupin's calm.)

GANIMARD (furious, to his men): Flatten this door! It's giving way. And you, Beautrelet, what are you doing? Shoot him! Kill him like a dog if he doesn't surrender.

(Lupin laughs.)

BEAUTRELET: I am disarmed, Monsieur Ganimard.

GANIMARD (completely crazed): Ah, Beautrelet, Lupin disarmed you?

LUPIN: Ah! You are disarmed? Fine. Here, take my revolver. Kill me if you dare.

(He tosses a revolver at Beautrelet's feet.)

BEAUTRELET (as he hesitates Lupin pins his arms): Go with God.

GANIMARD: What is happening? But this door! Men, what are you doing that you don't demolish it?

LUPIN: Ten to one that I escape, Ganimard.

HOLMES (appearing in the hollow of the triptych): I bet you don't.

LUPIN: Let's go! Fire, Ganimard. But be careful not to wound Beautrelet.

(He edges towards the triptych)

LUPIN: See how I escape.

HOLMES (pointing his revolver at Lupin): No, you don't. You're my prisoner, Lupin.

(Lupin turns from Beautrelet only to find himself facing Sherlock Holmes.)

HOLMES: Not a move, Arsène Lupin, or I shoot.

(At this same time, Ganimard and his agents finally succeed in breaking through the door.)

GANIMARD: Ah-ha! What do you say to this, Lupin?

LUPIN (calmly): Mr. Holmes—you've won this hand. What a man !

HOLMES (impassive): Thank you. (to Ganimard) Tie him up, Mr. Ganimard. You too, Mr. Beautrelet.

(They do.)

HOLMES: We were sure of winning, sure of you falling into our hands. You are very clever, Lupin; I am as much as you, perhaps more. And I win.

LUPIN (humiliated and supplicating): Will you permit me, Mr. Holmes? Jeannot is calling.

HOLMES (slowly): What? That's fine. Go ahead.

LUPIN (with anxiety): Please, Mr. Holmes. Do you know if Laura is all right?

HOLMES: Yes. You love her so much?

LUPIN: I adore her, Mr. Holmes. Her love will save me from crime—her love has regenerated me—and today—

GANIMARD: And today—nothing can save you from our hands.

LUPIN (violently opening a secret door in the chimney; at the same time, Jeannot enters; they detain him separately from Lupin.)

LUPIN: You are mistaken. See.

(Lupin disappears through the chimney door.)

JEANNOT (pleased): That's the end. He's escaped again!

CURTAIN

MYSTERIES & THRILLERS

M. Allain & P. Souvestre. *The Daughter of Fantômas*
A. Anicet-Bourgeois & Lucien Dabril. *Rocambole* (stage plays)
Guy d'Armen. *Doc Ardan: The City of Gold and Lepers; The Troglodytes of Mount Everest/The Giants of Black Lake; Doc Ardan: The Abominable Snowman*
Cyprien Bérard. *The Vampire Lord Ruthwen*
A. Bernède. *Belphegor*; *Judex* (w/Louis Feuillade); *The Return of Judex* (w/Louis Feuillade); *The Shadow of Judex* (anthology)
A. Bisson & G. Livet. *Nick Carter vs. Fantômas* (stage play)
André Caroff. *The Terror of Madame Atomos; Miss Atomos; The Return of Madame Atomos; The Mistake of Madame Atomos; The Monsters of Madame Atomos; The Revenge of Madame Atomos; The Resurrection of Madame Atomos; The Mark of Madame Atomos; The Spheres of Madame Atomos; The Wrath of Madame Atomos* (w/M. & Sylvie Stéphan)
Félicien Champsaur. *Homo-Deus; Nora, The Ape-Woman; Ouha, King of the Apes*
Jules Clarétie. *Obsession*
V. Darlay & H. de Gorsse. *Arsène Lupin vs. Sherlock Holmes: The Stage Play* (stage play)
Harry Dickson. *Harry Dickson vs. The Heir of Dracula; Harry Dickson vs. The Spider*
Séamas Duffy. *Sherlock Holmes in Paris*
Alexandre Dumas. *The Return of Lord Ruthven* (stage play)
Paul Féval. *The Black Coats (The Parisian Jungle; Heart of Steel; The Sword-Swallower; 'Salem Street; The Invisible Weapon; The Companions of the Treasure; The Cadet Gang); Gentlemen of the Night; John Devil*
Paul Féval, *fils. Felifax, the Tiger-Man*
Louis Forest. *Someone is Stealing Children in Paris*

Émile Gaboriau. *Monsieur Lecoq; The Casebook of Monsieur Lecoq*

Arnould Galopin: *Harry Dickson: The Man in Grey; Harry Dickson: Tenebras*

Goron & Émile Gautier. *Spawn of the Penitentiary*

G.L. Gick. *Harry Dickson and The Werewolf of Rutherford Grange*

Léon Gozlan. *The Vampire of the Val-de-Grâce*

Georges Grison. *The Heads that fell in Paris*

Paul d'Ivoi. *Around the World on Five Sous* (w/Henri Chabrillat)

Paul Lacroix. *Danse Macabre*

Jean de La Hire. *Enter the Nyctalope; The Nyctalope on Mars; The Nyctalope vs. Lucifer; The Nyctalope Steps In; Night of the Nyctalope; Return of the Nyctalope*

Rick Lai. *Shadows of the Opera: Retribution in Blood; Sisters of the Shadows: The Curse of Cagliostro*

Etienne-Léon de Lamothe-Langon. *The Virgin Vampire*

Steve Leadley. *Sherlock Holmes and The Circle of Blood*

Maurice Leblanc. *Arsène Lupin vs. Countess Cagliostro; Arsène Lupin vs. Sherlock Holmes (1. The Blonde Phantom; 2. The Hollow Needle); The Island of the Thirty Coffin; 813; The Many Faces of Arsène Lupin* (anthology)

Gustave Lerouge: *The Mysterious Doctor Cornelius* (3 vols.)

Gaston Leroux. *Chéri-Bibi* (stage play)*; The Phantom of the Opera; Rouletabille & the Mystery of the Yellow Room; Rouletabille at Krupp's*

Maurice Limat. *Mephista*

Jean-Marc & Randy Lofficier. *The Katrina Protocol;* (anthologists) *Tales of the Shadowmen 1-13; The Vampire Almanac* (2 vols.)

Richard Marsh. *The Complete Adventures of Judith Lee*

William Patrick Maynard. *The Terror of Fu Manchu; The Destiny of Fu Manchu*

Frank J. Morlok. *Sherlock Holmes: The Grand Horizontals* (stage play)*; Sherlock Holmes vs Jack the Ripper* (stage play)

Jean Petithuguenin. *The Adventures of Ethel King, The Female Nick Carter*

P.-A. Ponson du Terrail. *The Immortal Woman; The Vampire and the Devil's Son*

Georges Price. *The Missing Men of the* Sirius

Charles Rabou: *The Secret Bureau 1*

Antonin Reschal. *The Adventures of Miss Boston, The First Female Detective*

Norbert Sevestre. *Sâr Dubnotal vs. Jack the Ripper; The Astral Trail*

Eugène Thébault. *Radio-Terror*

P. de Wattyne & Y. Walter. *Sherlock Holmes vs. Fantômas* (stage play)

David White. *Fantômas in America*

Pierre Yrondy. *The Adventures of Thérèse Arnaud of the French Secret Service*